ACROSS THE GREEN GRASS FIELDS

ACROSS THE GREEN GRASS FIELDS

SEANAN McGUIRE

A TOM DOHERTY ASSOCIATES BOOK

NEW YORK

ACROSS THE GREEN GRASS FIELDS

Copyright © 2020 by Seanan McGuire

Interior illustrations by Rovina Cai

Edited by Lee Harris

A Tordotcom Book
Published by Tom Doherty Associates
120 Broadway
New York, NY 10271

www.tor.com

Tor® is a registered trademark of Macmillan Publishing Group, LLC.

The Library of Congress Cataloging-in-Publication Data
is available upon request.

ISBN 978-1-250-21359-4 (hardcover)
ISBN 978-1-250-21360-0 (ebook)

Our books may be purchased in bulk for promotional, educational, or business use. Please contact your local bookseller or the Macmillan Corporate and Premium Sales Department at 1-800-221-7945, extension 5442, or by email at MacmillanSpecialMarkets@macmillan.com.

First Edition: January 2021

Printed in the United States of America

0 9 8 7 6 5 4 3 2 1

FOR SERI AND CAYCI.
EVERYBODY NEEDS A HERD.

PART I

ORDINARY GIRLS

Hush-a-bye, don't you cry
Go to sleep, my little baby.
When you wake, you shall have
All the pretty little horses.
Dapples and grays, pintos and bays
All the pretty little horses.

　　—"All the Pretty Little Horses,"
　　traditional

1 THERE WAS A LITTLE GIRL

AT SEVEN, REGAN LEWIS was perfectly normal according to every measurement she knew, which meant she was normal in every way that counted. She wasn't short or tall, not skinny or fat, but average in all directions, with hair the color of straw and eyes the color of the summer sky. She liked spinning circles in the field behind her house until her head spun and the world turned deliciously dizzy, like it was humming a song she couldn't hear well enough to sing along to. She liked to read and draw and build palaces of mud, which she populated with frogs and crawdads and other creatures from the local creek. She loved her parents, and was only a little sad that so many of her friends had baby brothers and big sisters, while she had herself, and her parents, and a black-and-white cat named Mr. Buttons in honor of the three perfectly round black spots on his otherwise perfectly white chest.

Although sometimes her friends would come to school complaining about one or another horrible thing their brothers and sisters had done, and she would think maybe a cat named Mr. Buttons was the best sort of brother.

But most of all, more than anything else in the world, more than even her parents (although thoughts like that made her feel so guilty the soles of her feet itched), Regan loved horses.

She couldn't say exactly why she loved them so much, only that she did, and thankfully, "girls and horses" was enough of a thing that adults said it knowingly when they saw her doodling ponies in the margins of her math workbook, or when she went high-stepping around the athletic field like a quarter horse doing dressage. Loving horses didn't make her strange, and strange was something to be feared and avoided above all else in the vicious political landscape of the playground, where the slightest sign of aberration or strangeness was enough to bring about instant ostracization.

That was something adults couldn't understand, not even when they understood other things, like a love of horses or a burning need to go to the state fair, lest a lack of funnel cake lead to gruesome and inescapable death. They thought children, especially girl children, were all sugar and lace, and that when those children fought, they would do so cleanly and in the open, where adult observers could intervene. It was like they'd drawn a veil of fellow-feeling and good intentions over their own childhoods as soon as they crossed the magic line into adulthood, and left all the strange feuds, unexpected betrayals, and arbitrary shunnings behind them.

Regan thought it must be nice, to believe children were innocent angels incapable of intrigue or cruelty. She would have liked to believe that. But she had two major barriers between her and that happy ignorance:

Heather Nelson and Laurel Anderson.

The three of them had been the best of friends in kindergarten and into the first months of first grade. They had liked the same games and the same fairy tales, even if Laurel always got to be Snow White when they played princesses, and Regan always had to be the Little Mermaid, who couldn't talk or run or do the princess dance, because she didn't get to have legs until a prince came along and kissed her. They had liked the same colors and the same cookies and sometimes they all held hands at naptime, an inseparable circle of girls hurling themselves against the walls of the world.

But then, three months into first grade, Heather had come to school with a garter snake in her lunch box. It had been a beautiful thing, grass-green with golden stripes down the sides of its body, narrow as a ribbon, twisting and twining in Heather's hand when she brought it out at recess, making a strange, musky smell that was neither pleasant nor foul, but simply part of the great mystery of the snake itself. Regan had almost reached for it, and caught herself only when she saw the expression of profound, disapproving disgust on Laurel's face. She had taken an involuntary step backward, putting Laurel between herself and Heather, like the other girl could become a wall, a protective barrier, a way to escape the storm that was certainly coming.

"*What* is *that*?" Laurel had demanded, in the high, judgmental tone she normally reserved for bad smells and noisy boys.

Regan had looked intently at Heather, hoping to hear an answer that would somehow satisfy Laurel, that would make all this go away and put things back the way they'd been when she'd rolled out of bed this morning. But Heather had always been stubborn. This confrontation had been building for years, one small rebellion at a time. She had squared her shoulders, set her jaw, and looked Laurel in the eye, not flinching away.

"A garter snake," she'd said. "I found it in the garden when I went out to pick tomatoes. I think it was hunting beetles. That's what they eat when they're this little. Beetles and baby mice and sometimes grasshoppers. Do you want to hold it?" She'd thrust her arm out then, the snake still twined like a ribbon through her fingers, beautiful and somehow otherworldly at the same time, each scale like a glimmering jewel.

Laurel had recoiled and slapped the snake out of Heather's hand, a disgusted "ew" escaping her lips. Regan's gasp had been swallowed by Heather's cry of dismay as she lunged to recover her prize, followed by a squeal of pain when the snake, feeling ill-treated, bit her finger. She'd let it go then, turning to Laurel as it escaped into the waving grass of the kickball field, cradling her hand to her chest. Beads of blood had welled up on her index finger, and Regan had stared at them, transfixed.

This is what it costs to be different, she'd thought, the words clear and somehow older than the rest of her, like she was hearing the voice of the woman she was eventually going to become. She'd shuddered then, still unable to look away.

"Why did you do that?" Heather had asked, voice small and wounded. "It was just a little snake. That's all."

"*Girls* don't play with disgusting things like that," Laurel had snapped. "Regan, come on. We're going."

And she had grabbed Regan by the wrist and pulled her toward the school, leaving Heather alone with her blood and tears. Regan had looked back once, and that night she lay awake in her bed for hours, shivering with shock. She hadn't known what to say or do in the moment, or how to stem the tide of Laurel's rage, which had been so primal, so *fundamental,* that it was impossible to question. She knew even without asking that Heather was no longer a part of the trusted inner circle: she had performed girlhood incorrectly and hadn't instantly mended her ways when confronted with Laurel's anger. She was out.

That impression had been confirmed in the days to come, as Laurel walked through classes and recess and even lunch hour without seeming aware of Heather's presence, her hand locked firmly around Regan's wrist, tugging her into a future that had no place for girls who got their shoes muddy and played with snakes. Heather had tried, at first, to remind her old friends that she was still there; she had worn her prettiest dresses, the ones Laurel had approved of in the past, she had brought her nicest dolls to school, she had cajoled her mother into baking boxes of brownies which she offered to the other girls with shaking hands. None of it made any impression on Laurel, who had looked through her former friend as if she wasn't even there, tightening her grip on Regan's wrist like she was afraid Regan might also rebel against the box Laurel had drawn for them to share.

Eventually, Heather had given up on approaching them, her eyes going dull as the immensity of her transgression sank in. They had been a closed unit for so long that none of the other girls their age were looking for new friends—or if they were, they were also sensible enough to fear the wrath of Laurel, who had a way of destroying anyone who got in her way. Even some of the boys were afraid of her.

It was almost three months after the snake incident when the doorbell rang and Regan bounded down the stairs to answer the door. It would probably be the mailman with a bunch of bills and advertising circulars, but there might be a letter or a postcard or even a package, and even when those things weren't for her, it was exciting to be the first one to touch them. "I've got it!" she yelled, and wrenched the door open.

Heather, standing miserably on the front step with her mother's hand on her shoulder, blinked at her. Heather's mother was less visibly miserable, but her mouth was set into a thin, hard line, like she disapproved of everything around her. "Regan," she said in a tight voice. "Are your parents home?"

"Um." Regan took an involuntary step backward, away from the door, as if that would protect her from whatever was going on. She didn't like to attract the attention of adults who weren't her parents. Too many of them had strong ideas about how children were supposed to behave—stronger even than Laurel's, and Laurel left no room for negotiation. She looked down rather than facing Heather's anxious, unhappy eyes or the judgment in her mother's face. "I can get them. Do you want to come inside?"

"That would be for the best," said Heather's mother, and then she was inside, and then they were *both* inside, and Laurel was never going to let her hear the end of this. Regan took another step backward before spinning on her heel and fleeing down the hall, to the porch where her parents sat, sipping from tall glasses of iced tea while they talked about whatever boring things adults had to talk about when their children weren't around.

Her mother's head snapped up in alarm as the back door swung shut. She knew Regan wouldn't interrupt them without good warning, being sensibly concerned that she might be tasked with additional chores or—worse—walk in on them saying the sort of things that weren't suited for tender young ears. Regan knew she was fortunate to have parents who loved each other as much as hers did. Laurel's parents could barely stand to be in the same room for more than a few minutes, and Regan had been witness to several fights that should never have happened in front of a guest. So the fact that her parents still liked to murmur sweet nothings to each other was probably a good thing, but that didn't mean she wanted to hear it.

"Heather's, um, Heather's here," said Regan, twisting her hands like she thought she could spin her fingers into a rope that she could use to climb away from here. "With, um, her mother." She looked at her feet, not at either of her parents, who were already in the process of getting to their feet, putting their glasses of iced tea down.

"Do you know why?" asked her mother, who had noticed that Heather hadn't been coming around the way she usually did, but had been chalking it up to the kind of fights seven-year-old girls got into on their own time, strange and incomprehensible and vicious as anything. They were fights that solved themselves best when the adults stayed as far away as possible.

Cheeks burning, Regan began to shake her head. Then she caught herself, and nodded.

"Well, let's not keep them waiting," said her mother.

Regan led her parents to the entryway, where Heather and her mother stood, Heather's mother still holding fast to her daughter's shoulder. "I knew you couldn't know anything about this, or you would have put a stop to it," she said, without preamble.

"Put a stop to what?" asked Regan's father in a polite but mild tone. He'd never cared for Heather's mother, who seemed to think all the world's problems could be resolved by shouting a little bit louder every time she opened her mouth.

Heather's mother took a deep, slow breath, straightening as she did, like a balloon in the process of inflating. Her grip on Heather never wavered, and the taller she stood, the more Heather slumped, as if she was overwhelmed with the pressure of what was about to happen.

Regan shrank into the space between her parents, unwilling to meet Heather's eyes.

"Bullying," said Heather's mother, voice like stones falling into place in front of a tomb, locking its contents away from the world. Her hand spasmed before clenching tighter on Heather's shoulder. "Your daughter and Laurel Anderson have been bullying Heather since the start of the term. They won't let her participate in any activities they're part of, they've shut her out on the playground, and that Laurel didn't even invite Heather to her birthday party. My daughter is a sensitive child. I want this to stop."

"Regan?" Regan's mother turned toward her, expression solemn. "Honey, is this true?"

To her shock and embarrassment, Regan's eyes filled with tears. Her nose filled with snot in almost the same instant, and she tasted it on her upper lip, sticky and salty and childish. She was almost *eight*. She wasn't supposed to start bawling like a baby just because her mother sounded disappointed in her.

"N-n-no!" she managed, shaking her head so hard that tears splashed to the floor. "We're not *bullying* her. We're just not *playing* with her anymore!"

"Honey . . . why not?"

"B-because Laurel says she doesn't know how to play like a girl, and we're girls, so we only play with people who know how to play like girls do!" said Regan, and began, desperately, to explain what had happened the day Heather brought the snake to school. She didn't mention how beautiful the snake had been, or how much she'd wanted to touch it in the seconds between its appearance and Laurel's loud, vocal revulsion.

By the time she finished, Heather was crying too, although her tears were more subdued than Regan's, born less of panic and more of resignation.

"Don't you think it might have been wrong of Laurel to treat Heather that way?" asked Regan's mother. "There's nothing wrong with liking snakes and bugs, and I remember when we went to the fair and you held the python all on your own, not because anybody made you. Laurel doesn't sound like she's being a good friend."

Regan had known from the beginning that Laurel's love was conditional. It came with so many strings that it was easy to get tangled inside it, unable to even consider trying to break free. Laurel's love was a safe, if rigid, cocoon. Regan bit her lip and shook her head, unsure how to articulate any of the things she was feeling. "Laurel's my *best* friend," she said.

"Does that make it okay for her to push you around and tell you Heather can't be your friend anymore? Is that fair? You know there's no right way to be a girl. Destiny isn't reality."

Regan shook her head again, less fiercely this time. "No, it's not fair," she said miserably. "But she does it anyway, and she's my best friend. If I can only have one of them, I choose Laurel. Not Heather. I choose Laurel."

Regan's mother frowned, filled with a sadness as vast and impossible to articulate as it was when she'd been Regan's age and squirming under the thumb of her own playground dictatrix, because some things spin from generation to generation, and never really change, no matter how much we wish they would. She turned toward Heather and her mother.

"I'm sorry," she said. "I don't like this either, but refusing to play with someone isn't bullying. It's just being a less generous person than I would have hoped. I can't order Regan to be friends with your daughter."

"I told you, Mom," said Heather, voice despairing, and wrenched her shoulder out of her mother's grasp. "I don't want to be friends with them anyway. They're *mean*. I said I didn't want to come here. I want to go home." She turned and stomped out of the house, leaving her mother gaping after her.

"I really am sorry about all this," said Regan's mother apologetically.

"You should teach your child some better manners, before she gets herself into real trouble," said Heather's mother, in a clear attempt to have the last word. Then she followed her daughter out of the house, as Regan collapsed, sobbing, into her mother's arms.

2 THE COST OF BEING ORDINARY

TIME KEPT PASSING AFTER that, as time always does. Heather stayed away from Laurel and Regan on the playground and in the cafeteria, crossing paths with them only when school and its associated adults forced the issue. Years went by, first one and then two more. Laurel continued showing the sharp side of her tongue whenever given the opportunity, while Regan followed her through the world like a silent shadow, always careful to keep herself tucked inside the box Laurel had drawn, the one labeled "girl" in glittering, immutable letters.

Thankfully, Regan's horses, large and smelly and occasionally dangerous as they were, somehow managed to fit inside that box. She sometimes thought they would have been expelled from the box in an instant had Laurel ever bothered to learn anything about them, had she ever bothered to accompany Regan to her riding lessons or the stables. Horses had big, stompy hooves and large, terrifying teeth, and even with as much as she loved them, Regan had a healthy respect for the amount of damage horses could do if they decided they wanted to.

Plus, they stunk. Not so much when she was actually around them, and the reality of *horse* could drown out the less compelling realities of sweat and urine and horse poop, which came in piles as large as her torso, but as soon as the horses were out of the picture, and it was just her and the shower, or her and the shovel, the mammalian reality of them could be a little difficult to bear.

At least she didn't need deodorant yet. Her own mammalian realities were taking a while to make their presence known. It was frustrating at school, when Laurel and the other girls currently allowed within the inner circle started talking about training bras and periods with the worldly air of ten-, almost eleven-year-olds, and Regan had to hang around the edges acting like she was too cool to have opinions on shaving her armpits and whether Vivacious Vanilla or Luscious Lavender worked better for school-day antiperspirant.

She didn't like either one. She'd tried swiping them from her mother's side of the sink in the upstairs bathroom, and they both smelled like laundry detergent—yuck. Maybe if she smelled bad without them, she'd learn to have an opinion, but she didn't think so. Opinions were better reserved for things that mattered, like whether she should go to Karen Winslow's slumber party when it meant missing her Saturday evening riding lesson, or whether it was better to keep up her training and avoid being shut into Karen's bedroom with a dozen other girls, most of whom tolerated her only because she was still inexplicably Laurel's favorite.

Regan grabbed a shirt from the laundry hamper, folding it with sharp, efficient motions and dropping it onto the pile already on the bed. She knew why she was still Laurel's favorite. She was Laurel's favorite because she'd been there for the snake incident, and she'd learned, better than anyone could have possibly expected, why going against Laurel was a bad idea. Heather had never socially recovered from being cast out of the inner circle. She had a few friends who kept her company between classes—she wasn't *alone*—but she had never regained the vaunted heights of Laurel's approval. Regan had been there to see it happen. She had been there to understand just how quickly and viciously Laurel could take someone from beloved to beneath notice, and she had internalized that lesson remarkably well. She was still Laurel's best friend because she was willing to do the work to never lose her position, never be cast out of favor, never have to face the world alone.

As long as her horses didn't become the thing that made her strange, she'd be fine. She wasn't sure she could give them up, even for Laurel. No matter how many times her mother told her that girlhood wasn't destiny, she didn't think she could survive without Laurel.

But the other girls were starting to change in ways she couldn't copy, no matter how important it seemed. Their bones were migrating into new shapes, hips getting wider and waists nipping inward, some more obviously than others. Laurel was one of the "lucky ones," according to the girls who flocked around her in their ribbons and flounces, praising her developing breasts like they were something she'd accomplished through hard work and personal virtue, not hormones and time.

Regan grabbed another shirt, snapping it out with force before folding it neatly. She was being shut out more and more, referred to by the other girls as a child who should play with kids her own age, even though she was older than most of them. Breasts weren't a sign of maturity; they were just a sign of—of *breasts*! She wasn't even sure she wanted them. Some of the older girls at the riding stable talked about their breasts like they were wild animals that refused to stop attacking them, making jumps and dressage more difficult. They would have told her not to pray for puberty, if she'd asked them, which was why she never asked. They didn't have to thread the needle of normalcy the way she did. They hadn't been there for the incident of Heather and the snake. They didn't *know*.

Girlhood wasn't destiny unless you wanted it to be, and she had accepted her destiny wholeheartedly. Anything to be normal. Anything for Laurel.

Regan placed the neatly folded shirt on the pile, taking a calming breath in through her nose and out through her mouth. She'd have to go to Karen Winslow's stupid party. Staying home to go riding would solidify the idea that she was just a little baby kid and didn't deserve to be included.

It was a waste of time, and she'd hate every minute, but there wasn't any other choice. She'd been working so hard for so long to stay in Laurel's good graces. She wasn't going to lose her place now.

"Regan? Honey?"

She looked up at the sound of her mother's voice, unconsciously swiping a hand across her cheek. "Yes, Mom?"

"I just wanted to see if you were all right. It doesn't usually take this long for you to put away your laundry."

"I'm fine . . ." Regan looked at the welter of brightly colored shirts, socks, and underwear. The same sizes she'd been wearing the year before. Even some of the same actual clothes. She wasn't outgrowing anything. She wasn't *growing*, not the way the other girls were. She was getting taller—maybe a little faster than she should have been—but that was all. "Mom?"

Something about her tone made her mother freeze in the doorway, a thread of panic wending its way down her throat and filling the hollow behind her lungs, until it felt like there was no room left for anything beyond being afraid.

"Yes, Regan?" she asked, voice soft.

"Is there something . . . something *wrong* with me?"

Maureen Lewis had been waiting for her daughter to ask that question almost since she'd been old enough to speak. That didn't make it easier to hear; the weight of it was enough to rock her back on her heels, and the urge to flee the room followed close behind, until she had to grip the doorframe to keep herself from turning and running away. "No," she said, voice surprisingly steady, surprisingly clear, considering the situation. "There's nothing wrong with you, Regan. You're perfect. You've always been perfect."

Regan, who knew she wasn't perfect, frowned at her mother and said, despairingly, "But all the other girls are getting boobs and . . . and buying bras and deodorant, and Laurel just got her *period,* and none of that is happening to me. What am I doing *wrong?*"

Maureen frowned. "Do you want those things to happen?" she asked. "I thought you didn't want them yet."

"It doesn't matter if I want them or not when everyone else *has* them!" said Regan, voice peaking in a wail. "I'm the weird one again, and I don't want to be the weird one! Weird girls don't have friends!"

"If your friends would stop wanting you around because you're not exactly like them, they're not very good friends," retorted Maureen automatically, but somewhere in the back of her mind, she remembered the look on Heather's face when her mother had dragged her to the house to complain about precisely that problem. And what had she said? That she couldn't force anyone to be friends with anyone else? She had already known this day was coming, had known since before Regan was born. Oh, what a fool she'd been not to find a way to take Heather's side . . .

"Well, they would, and they're *my* friends, which means they're good for *me.*" Regan glared sullenly at her mother. "You know what's wrong with me, and you won't tell me. Why won't you tell me? Is it something really, really bad?"

"No. It's not bad at all. It's perfectly normal." Maureen rubbed her face with one hand. "Your father will be home in a few hours, and we'll sit down after dinner to talk this over as a family. All right? Is that good enough for you?"

Nothing could have been good enough for Regan in that moment. Nothing that wasn't an easy explanation of the changes—or lack of changes—in her body, or a solution for the growing distance she felt between herself and the other girls. But she was a good girl, and had been raised to show respect for her parents, so she nodded slowly, swallowing her protestations, and said, "After dinner is okay."

"Of course, sweetheart. You're our perfect girl." Maureen summoned a smile from deep below the panic swirling in her mind. "Now finish folding your clothes before your father gets home. You know I don't like it when we leave the laundry lying around long enough to wrinkle."

Regan scoffed, rolling her eyes as she reached for another shirt, and Maureen began to hope that maybe this wasn't going to be as bad as she had always feared.

3 PERFECTION IS IN THE EYE OF THE BEHOLDER

DINNER THAT NIGHT WAS baked chicken with green peas and cauliflower—one of Regan's favorites, a fact that didn't escape her as she settled at the table and filled her glass with sweet, cold milk. As an only child, she was accustomed to having her tastes catered to more often than not, but it was still worth noting, since her father's love of potatoes usually overruled her desire for cauliflower with every meal. Like her horses, that was a small weirdness she had been able to convince Laurel to accept, mostly by keeping it away from school as much as possible. Not a lot of opportunities for cauliflower in the school cafeteria.

Her father, a little subdued and worn out after his day at the clinic where he worked, sat across from her. He was a big man, with square shoulders and square hands, and always carried the faintest scent of fur and sweat on his skin. He wasn't the only large-animal veterinarian in the area, but he was known as the best, and his ability to coax even the furthest-gone foal into eating had saved a lot of horses since he'd opened his practice. Regan's riding lessons came at a discount because the owners recognized that having the local vet's only daughter utterly in love with their horses was the opposite of a bad thing.

Maureen had called him after her conversation with Regan, and he was braced for the coming discussion. He was the one who'd suggested cauliflower rather than potatoes. He somehow didn't think it was going to be enough.

Once they were settled, conversation died for a while, sacrificed in favor of silverware scraping against ceramic, and the soft, subdued sound of chewing. Regan ate more quickly than her parents, and sat with her hands folded in her lap rather than asking to be excused. Leaving the table might be taken as a sign that she didn't really want to know what her parents had been keeping from her. That would be low and mean of them, and she generally put more trust in their ability to play fair, but in the moment, she felt like she was being taunted with some great mystery that would put everything else into context. She was waiting for the world, which had been slipping slowly out of alignment over the course of the past year, to begin making sense again.

"Does anyone want seconds?" asked Maureen, voice high and artificially chipper.

"No," said Regan. "No one wants seconds. No one wants to keep sitting here, when we're supposed to be talking about what's wrong with me."

"There's nothing wrong with you," said her father, and quailed as Regan turned an imperious, oddly adult glare on him. In that moment, he saw what it was going to be like when she was grown and no longer required to bury her ideas and desires beneath those of her parents. She was going to be a force of nature, and woe betide anyone who stood in her way.

"We already had that part of the conversation, dear," said Maureen, pushing back her chair. "All right. Let's do this in the living room, like civilized people."

Regan tumbled from her chair in a very *un*civilized manner, nearly tripping over her own feet in her rush to move on to the next part of the evening. Her father rose more decorously, pausing to wipe his mouth. Hugo Lewis believed in the importance of table manners. He knew they were small in the greater scope of things, but they were concrete and predictable, and something to hold on to when the rest of the world spun out of control.

"We can clear the table later, come on, come on," said Regan, impatient as only a ten-year-old can be, and fled to the living room, taking a seat on the couch and practically vibrating as she waited.

She didn't have to wait long. Her parents followed her, expressions matched and solemn, shoulders almost touching. She looked from one face to the other and frowned.

"You've been waiting to have this conversation," she said, more confused than accusing. "How long?"

Neither of them answered.

"How *long*?" Regan repeated sharply.

"Since before you were born," said Maureen. Regan focused on her, bewildered, and Maureen continued, "When you're pregnant, you want to be sure everything's going the way it's supposed to. That means you have a lot of tests done, on both yourself and the baby, to check for signs that something's wrong."

Regan blinked. "So something *is* wrong with me."

"No, honey, no. There's nothing wrong with you. That's what all those tests told us. That we were going to have a perfect, wonderful, absolutely beautiful daughter. There was nothing wrong with you then, and there's nothing wrong with you now. You are the way nature intended you to be. Horse-crazy and not very interested in math and too fond of cauliflower for any ten-year-old girl." Maureen forced her tone into something light and airy, hoping to coax a smile from her daughter.

Regan's expression didn't change. "So what is it?" she asked.

Hugo sighed. "One of the tests we ran came back with some concerning results," he said. "It meant running more tests. More invasive tests. One of them gave us a snapshot of your chromosomes."

"And?"

"And your chromosomes are XY, instead of the XX the doctors expected to see when they ran the tests. You have what's called androgen insensitivity. That's why you haven't started puberty yet. It's why you may never start a standard female puberty on your own. If you hadn't shown signs by the time you turn sixteen, we were going to take you to see Dr. Gibson and discuss artificial hormone treatment."

"Sixteen?" demanded Regan, scandalized. The other girls were already starting to shut her out for being babyish and not maturing as quickly as they did. Sixteen was halfway through high school. Sixteen was practically an *adult*. If she had to wait until she was sixteen to experience things some of them were experiencing now, at ten and eleven, she'd never catch up. They would leave her behind forever, and none of them would look back to see if she was following. They'd forget about her.

Something else her father had said clicked into place, flooding her mind with a painfully bright white light. "Chromosomes?" she squeaked. "Aren't those the things that say whether you're a boy or a girl? I thought only boys had Y chromosomes. I'm not a boy. I don't want to be a boy!" Her voice, which had started out reasonably soft, grew louder with every word, until it was peaking and spiking like it was about to break.

"You're not a boy," said Maureen soothingly. "If you feel like you're a girl, then you're a girl. You've always been our daughter. You're just also part of a small percentage of the population who are considered intersex, meaning your body has its own ways of regulating things like hormone production. Some intersex people are more clearly a blend of what doctors would consider male and female attributes; that wasn't the case with you. There was no surgical intervention or modification after you were born—not that your father and I would have approved that if the doctors had wanted to do it. You are exactly as you were meant to be."

Maureen's words were calm and measured—too measured. Regan scowled at her.

"You're my *mother*," she said. "You're supposed to be making me feel better and helping me understand what's wrong with me, not—not reciting some Wikipedia article you memorized as soon as I got old enough to start asking questions! You're supposed to be on my *side*!"

"We are, pumpkin, we are," said Hugo, and sat next to her. "But you're right: we've had years to prepare for you to start asking questions, and that means we've played out this conversation in our heads a hundred times. It hasn't always gone well." He laughed wryly and shook his head. "But it's always gone. So this is hard for us too, just in a different way."

Maureen sat on Regan's other side. "Sweetheart, what matters most is that you understand there isn't anything *wrong* with you. You're exactly the way you're supposed to be. Some things may not come as . . . easily . . . to you as they do to other girls, and some things may need a doctor's help to happen, but you're perfect. There's no right way to be a girl. You're going to have a wonderful, perfectly normal life, and all this silliness about wanting to start puberty before fifth grade will seem like a childish obsession that was better off outgrown."

"Why are girls starting puberty so early, anyway?" grumbled Hugo. "I don't remember any of the girls needing bras before they were thirteen, and now it's like some sort of a race."

"It was always a race, dear, it was just a race you weren't running," said Maureen. "Ten is young, but it's not that unusual. There was a girl in my class who was wearing D-cups by the end of third grade."

Hugo shuddered. Regan, who didn't fully understand what that meant, just frowned.

"There's really nothing wrong with me?" she asked.

"Really," said Maureen.

"Really-really," said Hugo.

"I was born this way, and there's nothing you can do to change it?"

"We wouldn't change it if we could," said Maureen. "You're *perfect*. You've always been perfect, and you always will be."

Regan, whose ideas of perfection were closely linked to conformity, didn't say anything. She sat silently as her parents hugged her, first separately, and then together. She twisted her hands in her lap, tangling her fingers like the roots of a tree, and blinked back the tears threatening to spill over and run down her cheeks. She didn't want to cry in front of her parents. Only babies cried in front of their parents, and she wasn't a *baby*.

"Was there anything else you wanted to ask, sweetheart?" asked her father, letting go and leaning away from her, so he could see her face. He could see the brightness in her eyes, but he didn't call her on it. This was all a bit overwhelming for him, and it wasn't his body under discussion. It was understandable that she'd be a little upset.

"No, Daddy," she said, with a shake of her head. Then: "May I be excused? I have school tomorrow."

"All right, pumpkin," said Maureen. "Brush your teeth before you go to bed."

"Yes, Mom," said Regan, and slid off the couch, heading for the stairs. She didn't look back.

Her parents exchanged an anxious glance. "Did we do the right thing?" asked Maureen.

"We agreed to tell her as soon as she was old enough to

notice that something was different," said Hugo. "She noticed, she asked, we told her. I think it went about as well as it could have gone, all things considered."

Maureen sighed and leaned against her husband, closing her eyes. She wanted him to be right. She wanted everything to be all right. But she kept seeing the shock and betrayal on Regan's face. They had kept secrets from their daughter. Whether it had been for her own good or not, they had done it, and now they were going to face the consequences.

Upstairs in her room, Regan turned on her computer, bringing up Wikipedia. "Intersex," she typed, and began to read.

She was still reading an hour later, when her father knocked on the door and told her it was time to turn off the light. Her eyes were dry as she kissed his cheek and climbed into bed. Her mind was whirling, and she thought she'd never be able to fall asleep, but when Hugo flicked off the light, it was as if he'd flicked her off as well. She fell immediately into a deep and surprisingly untroubled slumber, which lasted all the way until morning.

4 SOMETIMES WE MAKE BAD CHOICES

REGAN SAT AT THE kitchen table, poking listlessly at her oatmeal, pushing raisins beneath the surface. Her schoolbag waited next to her chair, ready to be slung over her shoulder as she ran for the bus.

Her mother stood by the sink, rinsing the pot she'd used to make the oatmeal. "Your riding lesson today is with Caroline," she said. "You like her, don't you? You said she has a good sense of what you're capable of, even if it's not what you're doing right now."

Regan nodded, head bobbing up and down like a puppet's, and she shoved another bite of oatmeal into her mouth.

"Sweetheart, I need you to talk to me. I know we dropped a lot on you last night, but I need to know you understand it, and aren't going to be eating yourself alive all day."

"Huh?" Regan looked up from her oatmeal, spoon dangling loosely from her fingers. "Oh, yeah, Mom. I'm fine. I understand what you told me."

"I'm so glad," said Maureen, too relieved to question further. It had taken her a long time to understand what the doctors were trying to say; she was a smart woman, but this was her *daughter* they'd been talking about, and sometimes that had made it difficult for her to see things clearly. "You don't have to go to school if you don't want to."

"We're having a history test today. I don't want to have to make it up next week." Regan slid out of her seat. "The bus will be here in a few minutes. I love you."

"I love you, too," said Maureen, and watched Regan collect her bag and lunch and walk out of the kitchen. There was an odd finality in the moment, one that would come back to haunt her over the next six years, long after the search parties had given up combing the woods and the flyers had faded to illegibility in the store windows where they hung, endlessly hopeful, endlessly futile.

The screen door banged behind Regan as she left, cutting across the lawn to the bus stop. She was one of three students who were picked up this close to the edge of town, and the other two, the Ellery boys, were already there. As always, they ignored her, and she studiously returned the favor, staring blankly into the distance. Medical terms and confused, half-formed ideas chased each other around her head like untrained puppies, running into things and going sprawling, making it impossible to focus. It was almost a relief when the bus pulled up in a gout of exhaust and a rush of hot engine air, the door creaking open to admit the trio.

The boys sat up at the front with their friends, fellow princes of the playground. Regan slouched toward the middle of the bus, where a few members of Laurel's outer circle were already seated, passing scented markers back and forth, whispering, and playing with each other's hair.

At the very back of the bus, Heather sat alone. For a moment, Regan was seized with the almost irresistible urge to sit down beside her like the past few years hadn't happened, like they were still best friends, the kind of friends who could tell each other anything. Heather would understand what she was going through. Heather would pull a spare apple out of her lunch bag and start talking about how every flower was different and beautiful and wasn't that wonderful?

But she had treated Heather shamefully; she had chosen Laurel. So she sat with the other girls, who budged over to make room for her, even if they didn't welcome her, and folded her hands in her lap, staring straight ahead as the bus pulled away from the curb.

They stopped several times more to pick up more kids. On the third stop, Laurel got onto the bus, mincing down the center isle with quick, sure steps to plop down next to Regan, so close she was almost sitting on the other girl's knee. "Scoot *over*," she commanded, and Regan, long since trained to obedience, scooted.

"What's wrong with you?" asked Laurel, giving Regan a narrow-eyed look.

"Nothing," said Regan.

"Then why are you making that face?"

"It's just my face!" protested Regan. "I didn't sleep much last night. I had a big talk with my parents."

Laurel's nose wrinkled in sudden understanding, or

something that must have felt like understanding from the inside. "Did they decide it was time to teach you about S-E-X?" she asked.

"Why would they do that?" asked one of the other girls. "It's not like Reggie is ever going to have a boyfriend." Several of the others burst into wild giggles, like the cackling of a flock of crows. Regan curled further into herself, drawing her knees toward her chest.

Laurel, who could be cruel and could be petty and was frequently not a very good friend, held up a hand to signal for silence. The giggling stopped. With what sounded like genuine concern, she asked, "Regan? Can I help?"

And that was when Regan made the decision that would change her life forever, for both good and ill. She sniffled, and looked at the girl she'd called her best friend since kindergarten, and nodded.

"I think maybe you can," she said.

They finished the bus ride in silence, and walked together to the classroom. Fourth grade was taught by a single teacher in a single room, with the exception of PE and band, which happened in their own spaces. Some of the older kids said that when they reached sixth grade and transferred to the middle school across town, they'd change rooms throughout the day, with a different teacher for every subject. Regan thought that sounded very inefficient, and probably unpleasant, since there was no guarantee every teacher would like you, not when you had six different ones every single day.

But for now, it was one teacher in one classroom, and her

desk was next to Laurel's, where it had always been, and she was happy. She would have been happy if she could have stopped the world right where it was, so no one grew up, and there was nothing strange about her staying exactly the way she was.

Laurel, who could be like a dog with a bone when she thought people were keeping something from her, spent the first three hours of the day slanting sidelong glances at Regan and occasionally reaching over to tug her hair or swipe pencils from her desk in a bid for attention. Regan swatted her hands away and shushed her, eyes on the front of the room. She didn't want to get in trouble. Not when she was already tired, and her head felt like it was full of bees, and everything was wrong compared to the day before. The day before, she'd known who she was and what her world was going to be; she'd been so sure life had no surprises in store for her.

When the bell rang for lunch she jumped in her seat, so startled she nearly fell over. Only Laurel's hand grasping her sleeve and pulling her back kept her upright. Regan glanced at Laurel, thanks on her lips, and swallowed them when she saw the bright intensity in the other girl's eyes. Laurel had been scenting a secret all morning and now, like a hunting dog kept on the leash too long, she was ready to start biting at anything between her and her quarry.

"Come on," she said. "You promised."

And that was how Regan found herself at a table in the back of the library with Laurel, her lunch unpacked in front of her, the librarian somewhere up at the checkout desk, where she could keep an eye on the less obedient students, telling Laurel everything.

Maybe she wouldn't have done that if her mother had insisted she take a day off from school to think about what she'd learned and what it would mean for her future. Maybe she would have realized staying quiet wasn't the same thing as lying, and that while her body wasn't any sort of shameful secret, she was under no obligation to share it with anyone, especially not with a girl who had proven, over and over again, that she couldn't be trusted with anything that didn't fit her narrow view of the world. Maybe she would have realized that if there was no right way to be a girl, there was no wrong way either.

But Regan was accustomed to trusting Laurel, treating her like a vicious dog that wouldn't bite the one who held its leash, even as it barked and snarled at everyone else. Maybe that was why she missed the slow widening of Laurel's eyes, the slow paling of her cheeks, right until the moment Laurel pushed her chair away from the table and demanded, in a horrified tone, "You're a *boy*?!"

"No," Regan protested. "No, I'm not a boy, I've never been a boy, I'm a girl just like you, just one whose body's built a little differently—being intersex is perfectly normal, it's as common as being redheaded, and we have six redheads just in the third grade. I'm not a boy!"

"You *are*, though," Laurel insisted, taking a big step backward. "You line up with the girls during PE, and you come to slumber parties with girls—you've seen me in my pajamas!"

Her lip curled in clear disgust. "You're a gross, awful, lying *boy*!"

Regan leapt from her seat, shouting, "I am not! I'm a girl! My parents said so!" As soon as the words were out, she had to wonder if they'd been the right thing to say, or whether Laurel would care what her parents said about her.

Laurel did not. She took another huge step backward. "Don't you come near me! If you do, I'll scream!"

But they were already making more than enough noise. The librarian burst into the room, demanding, "What is all this ruckus about?" as she glared at the pale-faced Laurel and the shaking Regan. Laurel pointed at Regan, beginning to babble about liars and deceitful boys who wanted to get close to girls for wicked reasons. Regan ran.

She brushed past the librarian, who stared in bewildered shock as she made for the door. She ran out of the library, not bothering to wipe away the tears that now streamed freely down her cheeks. The scope of her mistake in trusting Laurel was just beginning to sink in, trickling down through layers of confusion and hurt.

She believed her parents when they said there was nothing wrong with her, because they were her parents and they had never lied to her. If they thought she was perfectly fine the way she was, they must be right, and since she'd been herself since she was born and it hadn't hurt her yet, there was no reason to think they'd start lying now. She'd just been confused and overwhelmed—was still confused and overwhelmed, if she was being honest with herself. This was a lot to try and wrap her head around at once, and reaching out to her best friend had seemed reasonable and logical. And it had been wrong, so wrong, so very, very wrong. Laurel looked out for Laurel before anything else, and Laurel's ideas about the world were black and white and starkly drawn, leaving no room for anything that didn't fit into her little boxes.

For Laurel, there *was* one right way to be a girl, and it was Laurel's way, always. Laurel believed in destiny. Laurel believed you had to be what people told you to be. And she'd almost convinced Regan to think the same way, that following Laurel's rules would be enough to keep her safe and ordinary. But that had never been the truth. Destiny had never been an option.

So Regan ran, and Regan kept running, barely slowing down when she hit the parking lot. She knew she'd get in trouble for leaving school grounds before the final bell, but she didn't care. Laurel was probably already rushing to the cafeteria to tell all the other girls what Regan had told her. Thinking Laurel would be capable of keeping anything in confidence had been the biggest mistake of all.

Regan ran across the street, into a small residential neighborhood. She'd been there before, trick-or-treating with Laurel and some of the other girls; she knew where she was going. At the end of the block there was a gap between fences through which a skinny girl who had yet to start the pressures of puberty could just fit, shoving herself through into an empty field filled with mustard grass and scrubby thorn bushes. She paused, chest heaving as she fought to catch her breath, then started to run again, loping across the field with the long, ground-eating strides of a child who'd been running for pleasure almost as long as she'd been able to walk.

At the end of the field was a slope, grass giving way to smooth, bare earth, hardpacked and streaked with reddish clay, shadowed by the branches of the nearby oaks. It angled toward the banks of a narrow creek, clear water dancing with catfish and crawfish. Regan slid down the slope on the sides of her feet, stopping at the water's edge, ragged breaths giving way to angry sobs that wracked her bones and burned her eyes and made her feel as if the entire world was shaking apart at the seams.

Bit by bit, her breath evened out and her lungs stopped burning, and her tears tapered off, leaving her feeling damp and oddly sticky. Frustrated, Regan swiped a hand across her mouth to wipe the wet away, tasting salt. She straightened, looking around. She knew this creek. It ran all the way through the woods; if she followed it long enough, she'd come out behind her own house. It would take hours.

She couldn't go back to school. Going back to school would mean facing Laurel and her army of giggling girls, all of whom would already have heard and accepted Laurel's version of the truth. It would also mean facing the adults responsible for her care, who wouldn't be happy about her unauthorized departure from school grounds. The damage was done. Why not go home?

Regan sniffled, smelling salt, and started along the bank of the creek, heading for the woods, heading for safety, heading for home.

PART II

HOOF AND HORN

5 THE DOOR IN THE WOOD

THE NAMELESS CREEK CHUCKLED softly as it ran along its bed of mud and waterweed and small, polished stones. The water looked cool and inviting, but Regan knew better than to take off her shoes and wade. Stepping into the water would kick up clouds of silt and make it impossible to see the bottom, and the last time she'd done that, she'd stepped on a chunk of glass big enough to go all the way through her foot. She'd limped home, bleeding, and barely made it to the back porch before the pain overwhelmed her. Well, she was miles from home now. Better not to risk it. So she stayed on the bank, watching the water tumble by, and enjoyed the shade of the trees and the sweet morning air.

If only she could stay out here forever, she thought, she could be happy. If she never had to return to school and confront Laurel's brutally triumphant, endlessly cruel eyes. If she could be absolved of the consequences of her own actions. If only, if only, if, if, if.

The world dwindled to the act of walking and the patterns of shadow on the ground. With the creek to guide her, Regan didn't need to think about where she was going; she only had to walk, and so she walked, following the water into the wood.

We should take a moment here, to talk about the wood. It was a small, tamed thing by the standards humans set for forests, long since boxed in on all sides by residential construction, homes and shopping malls and highways. But it remembered what it was to have been wild. It contained the seeds of its own restoration, birds and beasts and stinging insects, fish and frogs and small, burrowing things. If the boundaries were ever removed, the wood would be ready to spring back into its old wildness, for it had never been domesticated, merely winnowed down and contained.

Because it was tame, Regan could walk safely, without fear of meeting anything larger than a raccoon or a deer. Because it had been wild, she still caught her breath when she heard something passing in the brush, when a branch snapped for no apparent reason. Such is the dichotomy of forests. Even the smallest remembers what it was to cover nations, and the shadows they contain will whisper that knowledge to anyone who listens.

Regan shivered as something passed on the other side of a wall of trees, feeling suddenly less like the trees and the creek belonged to her, and more like an uninvited, potentially unwelcome guest. She began to walk a little faster, trying to figure out how far she was from her house. Not *too* far—this stretch of trees was far more familiar than the trees closer to the school had been. She'd wandered this far from her own backyard dozens of times before. She'd be home soon.

Her heart sank at the thought. She'd have to tell her parents what she'd done—that she'd told Laurel everything and then run away rather than face the consequences of her choices. And then she'd have to start convincing them not to make her go back to school, which was going to be hard, since she was pretty sure "told a secret to the wrong person" wasn't grounds for a transfer in the district's eyes. She didn't know for sure what *was*, but she knew Heather's mom had tried to get Heather transferred once it became clear that she was never going to regain the approval of her former friends. It hadn't worked. Heather was still there, on the fringes of the schoolyard, and only graduation was going to change things.

Regan slowed again, suddenly eager for her journey to take as long as possible. Maybe that was why the shape in the nearby growth caught her eye, and she stopped abruptly, sending a pebble clattering into the creek as she cocked her head and blinked at what was surely a trick of the light.

Two trees had grown around each other, branches tangling and twisting like the wicker of a basket. They looped in and out of one another's embrace, until they formed what looked almost like a doorway. That was interesting, but not unique; branches often grew together, and the shapes they made in the process could be remarkably architectural. She'd seen castles in the trees when she was little, castles and dragons and all manner of fabulous things.

But she'd never seen a doorway before.

Transfixed, Regan moved closer, eyes fixed on the shape. Unlike most of the optical illusions formed by the tangling of branches, it became *more* doorlike as she approached, not less. The twigs above it almost seemed to form words; she realized, with a start, that she could read them. "Be Sure," they said, in spindly, organic lettering.

Be sure? Be sure of what? Be sure she wasn't really looking at a door in the middle of the woods, since that would be ridiculous? Be sure that trees couldn't spell words in English, especially not words that were so clearly and obviously written? Well, she *was* sure of those things, as sure as she'd ever been of anything.

This was probably some high schooler's art project, something they'd set up so they could take pictures and impress a teacher.

Regan moved closer and closer still, thoughts of the fight waiting for her when she got home forgotten in the face of this marvelous new mystery. The doorway, such as it was, opened on a clear patch of ground, clay dotted with green moss and the small white flowers that sometimes grew alongside the creek. It looked perfectly ordinary, and perfectly harmless.

"I *am* sure," said Regan, and stepped through.

She wouldn't be seen again in the woods near her house for six long years.

6 WHERE THE UNICORNS ARE

THE AIR ON THE other side of the doorway seemed sweeter, cleaner, like it had been fed through some sort of filter that strained out every imperfection. Regan was too young to fully understand pollution and urban contaminants; she didn't recognize that what she was smelling was an absence of exhaust fumes. She could tell there was a difference, even though she knew it was silly to pretend two steps could have made any real difference in the air.

The little white flowers she crushed under her heels made a sweet perfume, crisp and almost spicy, sort of like fresh-cut ginger root. She sniffed again before kneeling and picking one of the uncrushed flowers, rolling its stem between her fingers. It didn't look like the flowers she'd seen elsewhere along the creek. It had the wrong number of petals, and the little speck of pollen at the center was a cheerful shade of pink, rather than sunny yellow.

Regan straightened, flower held between her thumb and forefinger, a shiver of unease running along her skin.

Maybe this was just an art project, but something about it felt wrong. She was trespassing on someone else's dream. She didn't want anyone trespassing on *her* dreams, and that meant she shouldn't be here. She turned back the way she'd come, intending to return to the path that would lead her home, and froze.

The doorway was gone.

The creek was there, and the hardpacked earth beside it, but it didn't show any traces of footprints; it looked like no one had ever walked there at all. The trees seemed denser and more tangled, and she couldn't see any houses or fences through them; this was a wood that had never known what it was to be penned in or encroached upon. Regan was familiar enough with this walk that she knew at once that the trees had changed. She stood, gaping, the flower falling from suddenly nerveless fingers.

She was still frozen when the unicorn stepped out of the trees. Its coat was a luminous white that seemed to glow against the shadows. Its head was shaped more like a deer's than a horse's, with a delicately pointed muzzle and large, mobile ears set to the sides rather than at the top. Its eyes were huge and liquid black, filled with glittering specks like stars.

But most impressive was the horn.

It was long, straight, and spiraled like the heart of a seashell, colored with the same mother-of-pearl shine. Regan had never seen anything so beautiful in her life. She couldn't even move enough to gasp, only stare, transfixed, as the living dream walked on golden hooves toward the creek. The unicorn didn't seem to realize she was there. Its ears were twitching, taking in every tiny sound around them, but its eyes were on the water. As Regan watched, it bent its long, graceful neck and began to drink.

Her heart felt like it was about to explode. Maybe this was her reward for everything that had happened; maybe she was being given the most beautiful death possible. Maybe—

"There you are, you stupid thing," bellowed a voice, louder than any voice Regan had ever heard, even though it didn't sound like a shout; it was just a big, booming voice. The speaker stepped into the open, and the reason for the volume became apparent. Regan's head spun like all the air had been sucked out of her body, leaving her dizzy and on the edge of passing out. A unicorn was one thing. A centaur was something entirely else.

And this *was* a centaur. From the waist down, the new arrival was a black draft horse with shaggy steel gray feathering around its vast hooves. It was at least sixteen hands tall—taller still once its human half was taken into account. Viewed from a distance, and without her horse half, the centaur's human half might have seemed like a muscular woman in her early twenties with hair the same steely gray as her tail and the fur around her hooves. Seen up close, she was gigantic, Amazonian, built to scale with her equine lower portion.

Regan had never seen a human being so large, and she still couldn't breathe as the centaur trotted over to the unicorn, grabbed it by the horn, and began pulling it back toward the trees. The unicorn went docilely, seemingly accustomed to this treatment. In a moment, it would be gone, and the most magical thing Regan had ever experienced would be over. She finally managed to pull in a tiny breath, making a faint whimpering sound in the process. The centaur froze, hand clenched tight around the unicorn's horn, and turned to look behind herself. Regan noted, almost dispassionately, that the centaur's ears were shaped somewhere between a human's and a horse's, as impossible as the rest of her.

None of this was happening. None of this *could* be happening. She must have fallen and smacked her head against one of the larger rocks that dotted the water. It was the only explanation for what she was—what she couldn't possibly be—seeing.

The centaur blinked slowly. Her eyes were steely gray, like her hair. *How nice that she's color-coordinated,* thought Regan, and swallowed what would surely have been a borderline-hysterical giggle.

"Human?" said the centaur in a wondering tone. It was the same tone Regan would have used to say "unicorn," had she been able to speak. "Are you a human? Am I standing in front of a *human*?"

Regan tried to pull in a breath that she could use to shape her reply. Her lungs refused to cooperate, and all she managed to do was make a faint, wounded wheezing sound.

The centaur let go of the unicorn's horn and clapped her massive hands, producing a sound akin to thunder. The unicorn flicked one petaled ear but didn't run. Regan swayed in place, more sure than ever that this had to be a dream. Nothing else made sense. Unicorns weren't real. Centaurs weren't real either, and if they had been, they wouldn't have been utterly enchanted by the sight of a human.

"You've just arrived, haven't you?" asked the centaur. "Bright and beautiful and brand-new, and I found you! Me, Pansy, found a human before someone else had a claim to chase. That's even better than bringing back a lost unicorn! A real human—you *are* a human, aren't you, not satyr or silene playing games with poor Pansy?"

"I'm human," whispered Regan. Her voice sounded dull, almost deadened. Still, now that she'd found it, it was willing to let her keep going, which she considered very sporting of it. "You're not real. None of this is real. Unicorns don't exist."

"But here I am, and here's a unicorn, and there *you* are." The centaur beamed. "Come on, human, let's go see the others. They're going to be even happier about this than I am."

Regan shook her head. "No. This isn't *real*. Centaurs are characters from Greek mythology. They're not named 'Pansy,' and they don't take lost human girls to see their friends. I'm dreaming."

"You must be a lot of fun at parties, if you always argue with your dreams," said Pansy, cocking her massive head. "Look, you have two choices: either this is happening, and you have the chance to meet Her Sunlit Majesty, which is a rare and glorious privilege, or this is a dream, and you have the chance to *dream* about meeting Her Sunlit Majesty. Either way, telling me I don't exist doesn't seem like a very good way to move forward. You want to take a deep breath and try again?"

Regan took a deep breath. Her knees buckled, and before she had a chance to react, she found herself sitting on the ground, crushing more of the little white flowers. She stared at Pansy. "Her Sunlit Majesty?" Her butt ached where it had hit the ground. She was probably going to bruise. She'd never been bruised in a dream before.

"Queen Kagami, ruler of the Hooflands for as long as I've been living. Longer, even. She's the first kirin queen we've had in, oh, ages, and ages."

"Kirin?" said Regan blankly. She had encountered the word in her reading, but not often enough to know what it meant.

"Like a unicorn, but smart as a person." Pansy sighed dreamily. "They're beautiful. Her Sunlit Majesty is supposed to be the most beautiful of all."

"Supposed to be?"

"I've never seen her. No one has. She's too beautiful for common folk to gaze upon; only the human will get to see her. I've never even been to the castle, because I'm just a herder, we don't have lots of opportunities to travel that far from our fields." Pansy brightened. "But now I can! Because *you're* here! Oh, everyone says only the human gets to see the monarch, but maybe they let the person who *brings* the human have a look as well! That would be a story to share a supper over. Me, seeing the Queen."

Regan felt like she was drowning. "This is real," she said. There were too many details she wouldn't have invented on her own.

Looking amused, Pansy nodded. "This is real," she

agreed. "You're human. You saw a strange door, right? And you went through it, and now you're here?"

"Yes," said Regan in a small voice.

"Welcome to the Hooflands," said Pansy. "We're happy to have you, even if you being here means something's coming."

"Something's . . . coming?" Regan scrambled to her feet, dusting crushed flowers and mud off the seat of her jeans.

"When a human shows up in the Hooflands, it means something bad's about to happen. You're tricky little things. Well suited to tight spaces, and thumbs. Having thumbs is sort of like having a magical sword no one can take away from you. It's destiny!" Pansy held up her hands and wiggled her own thumbs exaggeratedly. "Centaurs have thumbs, but we can't fit in a lot of places humans can, and we don't swim very well."

"Swim?" asked Regan blankly. She was starting to feel as if she'd been dropped into a conversation that had started long before her arrival.

"Sometimes swimming counts." Pansy grabbed the unicorn by the horn and tugged it toward her. "If you're done being shocky and convinced none of this is happening, you should come with me. Everyone's going to be so excited to meet you! Do you have a name? I can't just keep calling you 'the new human.'"

"Regan," said Regan unsteadily.

"Good name," said Pansy. "Well, come on, Regan. We can't stand here all day and expect the world to come to us." Still holding the unicorn's horn, Pansy began walking into the trees, back in the direction from which she had come.

Lacking any better ideas about how to cope with this strange new situation, Regan hugged her schoolbag to her chest and hurried after the centaur. Pansy smelled of clean fur and good, honest horse sweat, and that alone was enough to make Regan's shoulders relax a little. This was all strange and impossible and maybe not even happening, but horses were horses, and as long as there were horses, things would turn out all right in the end.

"So," asked Pansy, "what brings you here?" Then she laughed, as if she'd just said the funniest thing in the entire world.

"My feet?" ventured Regan. Pansy laughed even harder, her grasp on the unicorn's horn never slipping.

"I like you, human Regan," she said. "You're all right. I always thought a human would be stuck-up and weird, but you're almost like a normal person."

Regan blinked. "Why would a human be stuck-up?" she asked.

"I told you; thumbs." Pansy kept walking, her hooves clopping against the ground. "Thumbs aren't that common, and most of us that have them aren't as flexible as a human. We can't fit into the narrow places where humans can go, and we can't climb like humans can. We all know we're limited."

Regan, who had never considered that a centaur, with a horse's powerful legs and incredible speed, might think a human was better than them, blinked and walked on in silence. Ahead of her, the unicorn lifted its long, silvery tail and delicately defecated on the path. It didn't slow down or make any effort to cover what it had done. Regan wrinkled her nose. Manure was manure, even when it came out of a unicorn.

"I don't think you're limited," she said, stepping around the pile of unicorn poop as she continued to follow. In a softer, shyer voice, she added, "I think you're beautiful."

Pansy's laugh was as large as the rest of her. It boomed. The unicorn made a small bleating noise that sounded almost like an objection. Pansy laughed harder. "I can be beautiful and limited at the same time," she said. "Take unicorns. They're as beautiful as it gets, and they don't have the brains to come in out of the rain. They'll just stand there trying to figure out why they're getting wet and wait for someone to come along and fix it for them. There's nothing wrong with being limited, as long as you have people around to make sure those limitations don't get you hurt. Or drenched."

"Oh," said Regan, who had never thought of it that way. "I guess that's true."

"You know it's true," said Pansy. "Come on." She swept a curtain of branches aside and cantered through, leaving room for Regan to follow.

On the other side of the trees was a meadow that Regan *knew* didn't exist; it was too large, for one thing, vast and rolling off toward the horizon, covered in lush grass that was a shade of blue-green she was reasonably sure couldn't be natural. Patches of clover and buttery yellow flowers dotted the grass, but those were nowhere near as enthralling as the other things roaming the field.

Unicorns.

Dozens upon dozens of unicorns, in all shades of silver from cloud-pale to mercury-bright, their horns gleaming and their tails flicking away insects brazen enough to land on their glittering flanks. Most moved on their own, but there were a few small groups of three to six individuals, and even a few—Regan gasped aloud—a few babies. Their coats were more pearl than silvery, and their horns were short, stubby things, sharp as needles and ready to pierce the world.

Pansy shoved the unicorn she'd been leading away from her, giving it a slap on one perfectly sculpted flank. It shot her a reproachful look before trotting to the nearest patch of yellow flowers and lowering its head, beginning to delicately crop at the petals.

"They wander," said Pansy. "Especially the yearlings. Think they know everything there is about staying alive in the woods, when the kelpies and the hippogriffs will rip them to bits as soon as look at them. Nothing territorial likes having unicorns in their backyard. Too much potential for stabbing." She laughed again, startling some of the nearby unicorns, which trotted away. "But here I am, running my mouth like a filly, when you want to meet the others. Feel up to an adventure, human Regan?"

"Sure," said Regan, trying to sound as brave as she didn't feel. "Lead the way."

Pansy smiled, and clapped a hand on Regan's shoulder, and tugged her across the field, guiding her the same way she'd previously guided the unicorn. As for Regan, she went willingly, having no idea what else was left for her to do. They crossed the field of unicorns to a stone-and-timber building that Regan hadn't noticed before, sheltered as it was in the shadow of a copse of pines. Pansy opened the door, and both of them stepped inside, and were gone.

7 WHERE THE CENTAURS GO

PART OF REGAN WAS honestly surprised when she passed through the doorway and found herself in a long, smoky room instead of disappearing back to her own world. Doorways were suddenly untrustworthy; any one of them could be a portal into someplace altogether different, someplace as strange compared to this world of centaurs and unicorns as it was compared to where she'd come from. Her mind balked at attempting to imagine such a world, and so she abandoned the attempt in favor of gawking at her surroundings.

The room was easily twice the length of the stable where her riding horse spent his days, and similar in construction, with a beamed roof and rough wooden floor. Hooks on the walls held tack and sacks of grain and various tools, most of which she recognized, but a few of which she didn't. There were no stalls. Instead, the whole space was open, filled with smoke from the oil lamps burning on the long tables set up down the middle of the room, their surfaces laden with bowls of salad and platters of roast meat. Regan's stomach did a flip as she tried

to figure out what animals that meat could have come from. Given Pansy's casual handling of the unicorn, and the fact that the creature was apparently part of a flock to be herded, she could be looking at roast unicorn right now.

And then there were the centaurs.

It was almost difficult for her to focus on them; her mind kept trying to skip over them and go to the more familiar details, like the mud and straw on the floor and the faint scent of horse manure in the air. Those were things she understood. Even Pansy was a thing she understood at this point; she had encountered Pansy on her own, as a singular entity, and an exception was always easier to grasp than a category—but the others? They were too much.

There were eight of them, all female, all built on the same massive scale as Pansy herself, their breasts covered by laced vests, their arms bare and powerful, with biceps bigger around than Regan's thighs. Their coats came in every color of the equine rainbow, dapple and bay, chestnut and a silvery-gray that would have seemed luminous if not for the unicorns outside, reminding the world what "luminous" really meant. The oldest looked like she could have been Pansy's grandmother, with wrinkles and lines worked in the soft skin of her face and hair as white as a swan's wing. The youngest looked to be about Regan's age, smaller and lither than the others, with a gawky dun filly's body. She was, perhaps unsurprisingly, the first to drop the carrot she'd been idly munching, and point a trembling finger at Pansy and Regan.

"Human," she said, in an awed voice that was probably intended as a whisper, but which boomed through the room, as proportionately loud as Pansy's. "Pansy found a *human*. Mom! Pansy found a human!"

A dark chestnut centaur with elaborately braided hair walked over to the young one, clamping a hand down on her shoulder like the pressure enough would be a command to silence. "I see that, Chicory," she said, and unlike her daughter, she kept her voice low enough not to hurt Regan's ears. "Humans can speak. She heard you. I taught you better manners than that."

Regan's cheeks flushed and her ears burned with second-hand embarrassment as the young centaur drooped, pinned by her mother's hand. She shot Regan a look filled with shame, and it was so familiar, so essentially *human,* that Regan relaxed. These people might be centaurs, creatures out of myth and storybook, but they were *people*. They could be embarrassed by their own actions and by their overbearing parents. They weren't awe-inspiring. They were just people.

Regan reached deep enough to find a smile and pull it to the surface, offering it to Chicory. The young centaur blinked large brown eyes in evident surprise before smiling back, then grinning, her lips stretching wide to expose square, sturdy teeth as large as the rest of her.

A hand clapped hard on Regan's shoulder as Pansy boomed, "Her name is Regan. One of the wayward unicorns found her by the water, and I found the unicorn, and now she's here, with us! We have a human!"

The centaurs cheered, the noise so large in the enclosed space that it virtually had physical form. Then they rushed forward, surrounding Regan with the hot equine scent of their bodies as they bombarded Pansy with questions about where she'd found the human, had it been frightening, had there been any warnings before it happened. Chicory inched closer and closer, until she was close enough that Regan could have reached out and touched her, if that wouldn't have been impossibly rude.

Chicory's vest was made of pale leather. Regan thought of the unicorns and swallowed bile. It wasn't right to judge these people when she didn't know anything about them. If they were eating unicorns—and oh, she hoped they weren't eating unicorns—it would be more respectful to use every part they could, including the hides. Right? Right.

"Hi," said Regan in a soft, shy voice. No matter how hard she tried to think of the centaurs as people, not storybook creatures, part of her still regarded them with almost over-whelming awe.

"Hi," replied Chicory, and belched, as loudly as she did everything else. One of the other centaurs cuffed her in the back of the head, not hard, but casually, like she was swat-ting a fly. Chicory ducked her head and covered her mouth, giggling. Regan did the same, and for a moment, they were just two young girls surrounded by adults, united in a way that had been true since the beginning of time.

The adults were too preoccupied to notice when Regan backed away from Pansy's side, beckoning Chicory to fol-low. Even being their precious human didn't stop her from making her escape; like small, slight girls everywhere, she was well schooled in the ways of ducking under adult atten-tion. They would notice her absence eventually, but in the meantime, she could get to know the only person here who might be unguarded enough to honestly answer her questions.

The voices of the adults masked the clopping of Chicory's hooves. They weren't shouting—quite—but they all seemed to be trying to drown each other out all the same. Life with centaurs was a noisy life, that much was obvious, and Regan had to swallow the urge to clap her hands over her ears. She moved as far away as she thought was safe, to the end of one of the long tables, and stopped there, casting uneasy glances at the door, like it might reach out and grab her at any moment.

Chicory noticed. She frowned and asked, "Did you see something outside? Or are doors dangerous where you come from? Do they grab people who get too close?"

"Sort of," said Regan. "I was walking home from school, and I found a door in the woods that wasn't supposed to be there. I went through it because I thought it was funny. I wound up here."

Chicory blinked. "Don't you *want* to be here?"

"My parents are going to be *so mad*," said Regan. "I'm supposed to be home before sunset, unless I've already told them I'm having dinner at Laurel's house." She stopped, seeming to think about what she had just said, before bursting into silent tears.

Alarmed, Chicory looked over her shoulders at the adults. They were still talking amongst themselves, ignoring the girls. No one was going to yell at her for making the human cry. That helped a little. She'd never met a human before.

She didn't want to be forbidden to speak to the only one she had access to.

Turning back to Regan, she asked hesitantly, "Who's Laurel? Is she with a different herd? We don't have anyone here by that name, but if you tell me where she is, we can take you to her." It would be sad to lose the human so quickly. It would be even sadder to keep the human against her will. Humans were people too, at least according to the stories Rose and Peony told, and she didn't want to be cruel to someone who was a person. It wouldn't be like keeping a unicorn penned for its own safety. It would be like someone putting a rope around her neck, and that thought was enough to make the flesh on her withers crawl.

Regan shook her head, crying harder.

"You don't want to go where Laurel is?"

"N-no," managed Regan. She took a gasping breath, inhaling snot and tears along with the air, and coughed before she said, "Laurel used to be my best friend. But I said something she didn't like, and she doesn't want to be my friend anymore."

"Did you call her mother a swaybacked mule?" asked Chicory.

Regan sniffled and shook her head.

"Did you say she couldn't have any apples anymore? Or call her careless in her husbandry? Or insult her hooves?"

The idea of Laurel with hooves was ridiculous enough that Regan laughed as she shook her head a third time.

Chicory shrugged. "Did you say anything mean about her at all?"

"No," said Regan. "I told her a secret about myself. I can't tell you what it was. I don't know you well enough yet." And it had been hard enough to tell Laurel, who knew her and supposedly cared about her and who shared a basic vocabulary with her. Trying to explain chromosomes to a centaur—who might not know anything about the idea—seemed too big and exhausting to undertake, and she didn't think she could handle seeing revulsion in another person's face right now. Not after the day she'd had.

To her relief, Chicory shrugged and said, "That's fine. We just met. I'm not rushing to tell you all my secrets, either." It was such a refreshing change from Laurel, who would have demanded to be told everything immediately, that Regan nearly started crying again. Chicory must have seen it in her expression, because she looked alarmed and leaned over to pat Regan awkwardly on the shoulder. "It's fine. No one's going to make you go where Laurel lives. I can't promise you won't have to go through any doors. You wouldn't like being trapped inside forever. We go out during the day to herd the unicorns, and it would get really boring."

"Heh. Yeah." Regan wiped her eyes with the back of her hand. "My parents are going to be upset when I don't come home, was what I was trying to say. But the door I came through disappeared once I came through it, and I can't be sure a different door would send me home. If I have to be somewhere I don't belong, at least I can be somewhere that has unicorns."

Chicory snorted. It was a surprisingly equine sound. "Unicorns aren't anything special. They'd drown on a sunny day if we didn't bring them inside. And sometimes they get their horns stuck in trees and can't get loose, and we have to pull them free. Unicorn herding isn't all hay and horseshoes, and if you think it is, you're going to be real disappointed."

"They're beautiful," said Regan. "Sometimes that's enough."

"Sometimes," said Chicory, sounding doubtful. "Kirin are beautiful too, though, and they're *so* much smarter. Kirin are people. Unicorns aren't people."

"Where I come from, all those things are fairy tales," said Regan. "Centaurs too."

"I'm not a story!" protested Chicory. "Stories don't have to shovel unicorn poop."

Regan giggled. "Maybe not," she allowed. "But I've been shoveling horse poop since I was six, and it hasn't hurt me any."

Chicory blinked, frowning a little before she asked, "What's a horse?"

"Um." Regan hadn't been anticipating that. Finally, she shook her head, and said, "It doesn't matter. Are there really not humans here?"

"Not usually. Sometimes when something big and important is going to happen, a human shows up. Not always. When Queen Kagami grew up enough to take her family's castle back from the Kelpie King who'd stolen it from her parents, a human came out of nowhere and summoned rainbows and lightning from the sky to help her fight for her rightful place. Everyone says that human was very heroic, and when he was finished with his quest, he disappeared, and Her Sunlit Majesty ascended to the throne. There hasn't been a human since him."

"How long ago was that?"

Chicory shrugged. "I don't know. I wasn't foaled. Years and years and years ago. Maybe a hundred of them? I don't think my mother was foaled yet, either. Maybe her mother was, but Grandma Borage died two seasons ago." She didn't sound particularly sorry about it.

"Oh," said Regan, subdued. "I can't summon rainbows, or lightning, or anything like that. I can do my spelling worksheets, and skip a rope, and I'm a good rider, but if there aren't horses here, that's not going to do me very much good."

"Rider? You mean that thing where humans sit on centaurs' backs because their legs are too short and they can't keep up otherwise?" Chicory waved a hand dismissively. "It's good you already know how to ride. Humans have short little legs. We'd leave you behind in a blink, and that wouldn't be nice of us. Something would eat you if you went wandering alone, without your herd."

"I don't like the sound of that," said Regan.

"Most people don't, which is why they stay with their herds."

"It isn't offensive for me to ride you?"

Chicory shrugged. "Not if you ask first. We carry injured unicorns all the time. Sometimes it's the only way to keep the herd together. Or you could ride one of them! You don't have to ask a unicorn, since they're not smart enough to answer one way or another."

Regan's breath caught at the thought of riding a unicorn. She nodded slowly. "I think I'd like that," she said.

Chicory grinned. "See? You'll stay with our herd and be happy, and we'll have a human, and it'll be ever so good! We're going to have so much *fun*!"

After a pause to consider, Regan grinned and nodded her agreement. By the time the adults realized the two of them were missing, they were deep into the contents of a bowl of mixed fruit, chattering away like they had been friends for years. Which maybe, in a way, they had.

8 TIME AND TRANSFORMATION

CHICORY'S HERD CONSISTED OF nine centaurs, including Chicory and Pansy, who had been gracefully accommodating when it became apparent that Regan had a new favorite. According to Chicory, this was an average size for a farming herd; any larger and it got difficult to feed everyone, any smaller and it was hard to keep track of the unicorns. It worked for them.

Chicory's mother was Aster, whose sisters, Rose and Lily, were also with the herd. Clover and Lilac did most of the scouting, while Pansy, Bramble, and Daisy kept track of the animals. Daisy was a healer, and saw to the unicorns during foaling season, making sure the mothers were comfortable when it came time for the birthing, which required care to ensure the infant unicorns didn't accidentally gore their mothers on the way into the world. Wild unicorns were born with blunter horns, Daisy said, but these were domesticated unicorns, and they'd been bred to look as impressive as possible, which meant their horns were larger and sharper from the beginning.

The longhouse where the centaurs had been staying when they found Regan was one of many dotting the farmlands, each reserved for the use of whichever herd was currently grazing their flocks on the associated field. In addition to the unicorns, Regan saw centaurs tending sheep, long-legged deer, goats, and even fluffy, long-horned cattle; different herds had different specialties, including a primitive level of veterinary care for the beasts in their care. Daisy and the other healers did their best, but there was only so much they could manage with the level of technology they had access to. Regan asked once about antibiotics, and got stared at like she was trying to cast spells in a language none of them had ever heard before.

Pansy repeated her offer to take Regan to the Queen several times. The law of the Hooflands said all humans must be presented to the king or queen, but there was nothing in the law that said exactly *when* it had to happen. Regan demurred, saying she preferred to stay with the herd, and the centaurs listened to what she had to say. It was an amazing change from home, where she was sometimes catered to but never really listened to about important decisions.

They left the longhouse after a week, when the unicorns had grazed out their field. By that time, Regan had come to grips with the fact that she was going to be very, very late getting home from school; that her parents had, most likely, decided she was missing, and put up flyers at the grocery store. She was young enough yet that the idea of anything further didn't occur to her; she didn't realize they would be terrified, or that her father might be questioned in the matter of her disappearance, coming as it had in the wake of another student accusing Regan of being a boy who'd been attending school in girl's clothing for years. No one would question Laurel's accounting. After all, Regan wasn't there to defend herself. She was far, far away, learning to sleep in beds of woven grass, gradually losing her awe over unicorns, climbing trees for late summer apples, and sharing blackberries with the centaur girl who was her new best friend.

The Hooflands were warm and temperate; it rarely rained, but when it did, the storms lasted for days, lighting up the horizon with lightning, shaking the walls with thunder. Pansy's dire proclamation proved to be just shy of true; the unicorns would run from thunder and then stand in the middle of the field with their heads tilted back and mouths open, watching the lightning. They would have drowned if they hadn't been herded into the longhouse, where they filled the room with heat and the wet animal smell of sodden equine. More of Regan's awe died during the first storm. It was hard to be dazzled by a wet, muddy unicorn that was attempting to eat your mattress.

And time marched on. Regan had been with the herd for the better part of a season when foaling time arrived. It seemed like all the unicorn mares had gotten pregnant at the same time, and Daisy's hours were filled with constructing nests of hay and sweetgrass and luring gravid unicorns into them, or sending Pansy off to look for a mare who had decided to go into the wild and give birth on her own. Regan and Chicory were frequently called to help both Daisy and Pansy at first, but as the season went on, Daisy requested

Regan more and more often. Regan's hands were smaller than any of the centaurs', and she was better built for kneeling, and she could handle fine details of care that Daisy herself was no longer capable of.

The first time Regan was called to assist with a birth, Pansy boomed with laughter and slapped her on the shoulder so hard she staggered. "I told you. Thumbs! It's all about the thumbs with you humans." And then she cantered off to round up the unicorns, who were closer to a gully than was good for them.

That night, Regan helped Daisy ease a foal with a dappled coat and a needle-sharp horn the length of Regan's own index finger into the world, wiping him clean before settling him beside his mother, who lowered her head and shook her horn at the interlopers. Daisy laughed, swatting her on the flank.

"Be quiet, you old thing," she said. "My apprentice is only here to help, and she got you a fine boy instead of an early grave. Appreciate what you have and let yourself be happy."

"Apprentice?" Regan asked, voice trembling.

"If you want to be," said Daisy. "You're our human, and you don't have to work if you don't want to; just having you with us is a sign of status in the eyes of the other herds, and I know you must go to the Queen in her castle when it's time. You can be indolent and foolish until then, if it's what makes your heart happy. But I don't believe it is. You're too slow to scout and too small to handle the stallions, so you can't work the herd. Yet you volunteer whenever there's something you think you *can* do. This is something you can do. You can help me save lives. I can teach you."

"What happens if a door catches me?" asked Regan, voice suddenly small.

Daisy sighed, putting one large hand on the girl's shoulder. "They're not predators, child, not like the kelpies. They won't chase you down to break your bones and rend your flesh. When your time to return to where you came from arrives, the door will find you and it'll be up to you whether or not you go through."

"But everyone says humans disappear after they do whatever they came here to do," protested Regan, voice getting louder. The centaurs never scolded her for yelling. Her normal speaking voice was soft enough compared to theirs that they heard almost everything she said as if it was a whisper. "I don't want to be your apprentice and then disappear on you! That's not fair!"

"Peace, child, peace." Daisy offered her a smile. "Any of us could disappear at any time. Landslides, predators, even illness, they come for us all if age doesn't get there first. So you can be my apprentice, and I'll teach you as much as I can before you leave us, and when you do leave us, I'll find someone else who wants the things I have to offer. It won't be Chicory. She has no grace for it, and no desire to be tied to the herd for all her days. Maybe at the Fair we can barter for another girl who's interested in the healing arts, if you feel it necessary."

"The Fair?" asked Regan.

"We'll go there as the year turns, before you and Pansy travel to the Queen," said Daisy, picking up her basket of herbs and balancing it on her withers. "We'll bring the stock to sell what we can, since the flock can't be allowed to get too large. We'll visit our husbands, those of us who have them, or the local boys, if we don't. And some herds will have grown too large, and may be looking to send their daughters off to learn honest trades. We could sustain a few more mouths."

Regan blinked. This was the first she'd heard of husbands, and while she'd wondered why all the centaurs were female, she had never felt she could ask before. "Husbands?" she asked.

Daisy clucked her tongue. "Go tell Pansy the foal's out, and the mare survived. You're too young to speak of husbands. Go now, go."

Regan, who was generally obedient when she lacked reason not to be, turned and ran for the longhouse. The more time she spent with the centaurs, whose walking pace was her jog, the harder she found it to do anything slowly. So she ran, and Daisy smiled, watching the girl go.

It had been so long since there was a human in the Hooflands. She didn't like to consider what might be ahead of them that was bad enough to require human intervention. Humans were heroes and lightning rods for disaster, and none of the stories she'd heard about them when she was a filly had ended gently for them, or for the people around them. Aster had always been careful to tell Chicory the most hopeful of the human stories, the ones where the humans did their grand deeds and disappeared, presumably going back where they came from, but Daisy's own mother had been less circumspect, and she knew where most of the humans had gone when their battle ended—into the ground. She couldn't possibly say whether the same fate waited for Regan—it was too soon for that, and she'd never heard of a human hero as young as Regan was, or as eager to please—but the girl was more likely to find her own doom than a doorway home. In the meantime, the herd would care for and tend to her, and part of that caring was keeping her busy enough that her thoughts didn't devour themselves alive. She was a child, far from home, surrounded by members of a species that wasn't hers. It would have been understandable for her to fall into despair. The fact that she hadn't was barely shy of a miracle, and one more piece of proof that humans could do anything when they put their minds to it.

Daisy sighed, one hand stabilizing her basket, and started plodding toward the longhouse. They were going to protect and nurture the girl as long as they could, keeping her safe from a world that would have happily destroyed her. Regan still viewed anything with hooves as a potential friend, looking on them with joy and wonder, no matter how many times she was warned about the kelpies and the perytons and the bat-winged pterippus. It made Daisy wonder how many humans they had missed, children who had stumbled through a door without someone like Pansy nearby to save them from their own adventure. Regan could have been lost before she was ever found, if the kelpies had been only a little bit hungrier on the day she'd crossed over.

It was the sort of thought that benefitted no one. Daisy shook it off and walked faster, following Regan's tracks to the longhouse.

Inside, Regan and Chicory were playing an elaborate game of tag, both laughing. Chicory was faster, but Regan was nimbler, and managed to evade being tagged by jumping off a table and grabbing the lowest of the ceiling beams, dangling. Chicory squealed and grabbed at her legs while Regan thrashed.

Daisy cast an indulgent smile at the girls as she trotted to where Aster, Rose, and Lily were repairing one of the nets they used to subdue the stallions when they grew too aggressive. "Foal's here," she said. "Good, strong colt. He'll be a fine stallion someday."

"Regan told us," said Aster, and tied another careful knot in her mending. "She said you've asked her to serve as your apprentice."

"So I have," said Daisy.

"I always thought Chicory—"

"Chicory is a fine, clever girl, and you should have all the pride in her that you can carry. Take her to meet her sire when we go to the Fair. She's earned the right." Daisy scowled as Aster turned her face away. "If you didn't want him to be a father, you shouldn't have chosen him."

"It wasn't his fatherhood potential she was looking at," murmured Rose. Lily snickered, stopping only when Daisy turned her scowl on the pair.

"And you! Neither of you has an aversion to men or motherhood, and you're both young. The herd needs replenishing."

"So we take apprentice contracts," said Rose.

"Or you take husbands at the Fair and you foal in the

spring," said Daisy. "We won't have a human forever, however much we might wish we would. Humans don't work that way." She cast a mournful glance at the two children chasing each other around the beam. "Soon she'll be gone, and her clever hands with the rest of her. We need to build the herd, or Chicory will be an elder surrounded by the foals of strangers one day. That isn't fair to her."

The other women were briefly quiet, considering their own childhoods, and how lonely they would have been if they'd had no one but adults and apprentices to share them with. Finally, Lily nodded.

"Come the Fair, we'll go courting," she said.

"Good," said Daisy, and the children played, and the time passed, and it was far too late to take any of it back.

9 OFF TO THE FAIR WITH BANGLES AND BEADS

ANOTHER SEASON PASSED, ONE day at a time, so quickly that Regan forgot she was meant to be worrying about her parents, far away from her and probably worried about where she was. Getting to them would mean risking a door, if a door could even be found, and she was still leery of those, even when they were solid, ordinary, and familiar, like the doors of the longhouses that provided safe haven for the herd as they moved closer to what she now recognized as the Fair.

One of the old stallions broke his leg and had to be put down, because there was no better way to ease his suffering. The horns of unicorns had no healing power after all. There was meat on the table that night for the first time in months, and this time, to honor the unicorn's sacrifice, Regan ate with the rest of them. It was sweet and tender on her tongue, surprisingly so, and Pansy laughed at the expression on her face.

"You thought we raised these things for their charming personalities?" she asked. "They give good milk and they make decent cheese, but they do their best work on the dinner table."

Regan, red-faced, ducked her chin and didn't answer.

Time kept passing. They moved to another pasture; the mares who had belonged to the old stallion for the longest stopped looking for him, and settled to focusing on the latest crop of foals, who were growing up fast. Regan continued to study under Daisy, learning which herbs could ease a pain or break a fever, and which mushrooms could be pressed for good medicine, and which ones would kill in a mouthful. She still spent most of her time with Chicory, the two sinking deep into the sort of friendship that only ever seems to come for young things.

Regan grew taller, arms and legs lengthening as if they were trying to catch up with Chicory herself. She dropped from a tree onto Chicory's back while the adults were rounding up the flock, and Chicory laughed as she broke into a gallop, the two girls forming one body as she raced across the meadow. Prior to that, when they moved from place to place, Regan had ridden either Pansy or Daisy. After that, she rode Chicory almost exclusively, and the two of them took to sleeping in a tangled heap of limbs and hair and noisy sighs. The adults all agreed, without a word exchanged, that if Regan's act of human heroism was to give comfort and friendship to one lonely centaur girl, they would consider her efforts to have been well spent.

And then, in what felt like the blinking of an eye or the rising of a single sun, it was time for the Fair.

Chicory and Regan were ordered down to the pond,

which had been verified clear of either kelpies or large snapping turtles, to scrub themselves until they shined. When they returned from their ablutions, dripping, they were met by Aster and Daisy, who ordered them to sit in the corner of the longhouse and stay as clean as possible. The rest of the herd was already absorbed in rounding up the unicorns, chasing them into a temporary paddock and guiding them down the path toward the distant promise of the Fair.

"Both of you will behave today," said Aster, in a tone which left no room for argument. "You will obey your elders. Chicory, you will stay with Regan at all times, and if anyone attempts to touch her, you will stop them."

"Even if they're my elder?" asked Chicory nervously.

"Even then," said Aster. She turned her gaze on Regan. "We won't deny you the Fair, any more than we'd force you to go and see the Queen before you must. You have every right to see and experience and enjoy the world you're going to be asked to save. See its wonders. Taste its bounty. But understand that there may be some there who think you deserve better than a roving herd of unicorn farmers, and want you to go with them. Some may not want to take 'no' for an answer. You'll need to be alert and aware of your surroundings at all times."

Regan blinked slowly. "Won't you be there?" she asked.

"No. I'll be with Chicory's father, my husband, and the others intend to go courting. There may be foals or marriages from this Fair, which is just more reason we must go, even with you in our custody. Do you understand?"

Regan, who still had only the vaguest understanding of

how the centaurs arranged themselves socially, and who had yet to see a male centaur, nodded anyway. It was the sort of question adults expected to have answered in the affirmative, and asking questions wouldn't help anything.

Aster looked relieved. "Good. I'm glad." She trotted over to Chicory, gripping the sides of her daughter's head. "You are a worthy daughter, and more than suited to being companion to a human. You'll do me proud at the Fair, and your father will praise your name." She planted a kiss on Chicory's forehead.

"Ew, Mom." Chicory wiped the kiss away with one hand. "We'll behave ourselves. We're not babies."

"Regan is, though, where the Fair is concerned."

Regan frowned. "I've exhibited at the State Fair before," she said. "This can't be that different."

"I don't know what a State Fair is, but I'd wager it's very different from the Fair," said Aster. "Come along. The others will be almost there." She trotted out of the longhouse. Chicory and Regan exchanged a look, before Regan shrugged and boosted herself onto Chicory's back, settling easily. Chicory trotted after her mother, breaking into a canter once they were safely outside, and there was room to run.

On an ordinary day, room to run and no chores to do would have led to Chicory racing away across the fields while Regan held on for dearest life, the centaur's hair slapping the human repeatedly in the face, both of them laughing with delight at the simple joy of being alive, and young, and together in a world that was better when not experienced in isolation. Anything with enough brain to know itself as an individual will reach out to others, looking for companionship, looking for other eyes with which to see the world. Regan had never really been lonely—Laurel had always been there to provide companionship, if not true support—but she had still been alone. In Chicory, she had finally found a friend who liked her for who she was, not for how well she fit an arbitrary list of attributes and ideals. Chicory, on the other hand, had been lonely, growing up surrounded only by adults, with no one her own age to share her questions and concerns, or who was experiencing the world at the same rate she was. Together, they were perfect. It was no surprise to anyone who saw them for more than a few seconds that they were inseparable.

None of the adults had waited, not even Aster, although the dust from her passage hung in the air, marking the direction she had gone. Regan tightened her grip on Chicory's shoulders, anticipating what would happen next. Chicory broke into a gallop, hooves chewing up distance like a unicorn chewed its cud, and Regan whooped, delighted. Chicory wasn't as fast as she'd be when she was grown, but she was faster than any human, and sitting astride her back sometimes felt like the next best thing to flying.

Despite their head start, the rest of the herd was no match for an excited preteen afraid of missing out on the most exciting event of the season. Chicory caught up to them in short order, slowing to prevent her hoofbeats from frightening the unicorns, who were already uneasy after being curried, scrubbed, and rounded up for the long walk away from their familiar fields. The road to the Fair was hard-pressed dirt, worn smooth by generations of marching hooves, long and gently winding.

Chicory passed her mother and the others, trotting up to the front of the group and falling into an easy canter next to Pansy, who looked over and smiled indulgently at the two girls.

"Don't you look fine today?" she asked. "Any special occasion?"

"The Fair," said Chicory, indignant as only an almost-teen being teased by an adult can manage. "I'm going to get baked apples and share them with Regan."

"So long as you share," said Pansy. She reached into her vest, producing two small leather bags with bulging sides, and passed them over. "You both worked with the flock this season. Here's your share of the profits so far."

Chicory stared at Pansy with wide, round eyes, clutching the pouch to her chest. Regan, who still wasn't completely sure the centaurs *used* money, undid the knot on hers and peered curiously inside at the flat copper coins.

"They're like really big pennies," she said in a bewildered tone. "What's this for?"

"People expect you to pay for things at the Fair," said Pansy. "Chicory's old enough to go off on her own this year, and you're the same age, so we can't expect you to sit idly by while she's running around getting into mischief. Not that we want you sitting on your own, and we all have things to be doing."

"Husbands?" asked Regan, tying the bag to the worn, tattered waistband of her jeans. They had been perfectly good for wearing to school once or twice a week. They were woefully unsuited to being her only clothes for months on end, and had been coming apart at the seams even before her most recent growth spurt stretched her upward, leaving inches of dirty ankle visible.

"That's none of your concern, either of you, not until you're much, much older," said Pansy. "I'll not be courting, anyway. I need to get these beasts to the marketplace, and see how many of them we're to trade for supplies to sustain ourselves over the winter yet to come. You worry about baked apples and pheasant pies for your stomachs, and you let us worry about the things that shouldn't trouble you yet."

"Yes, ma'am," said Chicory, and "Yes, Pansy," said Regan, and Pansy smiled, content as only an adult who believed she had addressed all the possible problems of the children in her care could be.

Regan had no concept of how much money she had, and so she put it out of her mind in favor of gazing at the landscape around them, trusting Chicory to know where she was going. They were no longer in the tree-shrouded fields she had grown accustomed to, and were passing through what looked like actual farmland, ripe and rich with artichokes and strawberries and other greens she couldn't identify. Off in the distance stood a windmill, and she couldn't help but think it must be manned by something other than the centaurs, whose size would make it awkward for them to climb the stairs. Birds soared overhead, their wings wide and brightly colored.

Every day, the Hooflands found another way to remind

her that this wasn't the world she came from, and that she'd never truly belong here, no matter how long she stayed. That was a good thing in some ways, because she *did* want to go home, she *did* want to return to her parents, who had always treated her well, and who had to miss her something awful. She'd never been away from them for longer than the span of a stay at summer camp before, and up until now, she'd been able to partially pretend this was just another kind of camp, wilder and wider and more like her dreams than the others, but summer camp all the same. Only, the summer was coming to an end, replaced by the chill and gathering autumn, and when it was entirely gone, could she really pretend this was a temporary thing?

One day, she'd have to wake up and face the reality that she was a runaway, that her parents were probably mourning her, sitting awake through the long hours of the night, terrified that the next time the phone rang, it would be the police telling them her body had been found, that Laurel was spreading rumors and lies all over the school about why Regan had felt the need to run, that even when she did go home, things would never be the same. And maybe that wasn't the worst thing ever. Maybe it was time for change. Everything changes, given the right catalyst. She'd changed already, compared to the girl she'd been when she saw the door of twisted branches and shadows.

The girl she was now would be a better friend to Heather. She knew that. She had brought a unicorn into the world; she had apprenticed and was apprenticing to a centaur healer. Her ideas about "normal" had changed dramatically in just a few months, and she couldn't imagine a world where they'd change back. She was sure Laurel would make fun of her for spending time with Heather again, but what did that matter? Laurel's words had been enough to hurt her before, when she'd thought the world she knew was all there was. She knew better now. The world was bigger now. She was bigger now, and that made all the difference.

Bit by bit, the fields fell behind them, replaced first by livestock—goats and sheep, and the fluffy cows she'd seen before, grazing with their muzzles to the close-cropped ground. Then the livestock fell away, and it was wheat as far as the eye could see, stretching toward forever, enveloping the few trees foolish enough to grow in its path. Regan shivered and pressed closer to Chicory, who glanced over her shoulder and offered a slight smile.

"We're almost there," she said. "Fair has to be a trek for everyone, or it would never be able to be even as close to um, well, fair as it manages to be. Everybody travels."

"Why does it have to be fair?"

Chicory shook her head. "It just does. And it keeps the herds from fighting for the fields nearest the Fair. Because we move around all year long, we'd disrupt the harvest and the grazing patterns of the flocks if we tried to end the season as close to the fairgrounds as possible. So everyone travels. Those fields are in the keeping of the Queen, and no one works them."

"Huh." It seemed like a reasonable solution to an unreasonable situation. Regan shrugged, leaning back on her hands, so her weight was resting as much on Chicory's haunches as on her midsection. "You've been to the Fair before, yeah?"

"Every year since I was a foal," said Chicory. "This is the first year I'll be allowed to go off without an adult, I guess because you're here to keep me company. Means it's the first year Mama will be able to go see my father, too. I bet she's missed him."

"Back where I come from, mothers and fathers live together most of the time. Unless they're divorced."

"What's 'divorced' mean?"

"It means they were married and now they're not anymore, so their kids get double Christmas."

"Oh," said Chicory blankly. "What's Christmas?"

It was rare to run into two unfamiliar concepts in one conversation anymore; they'd had long enough to talk about whatever came to mind that they seemed to have covered every subject two clever, eager little girls could cover. Regan blinked, leaning farther back, trying to find her way to the answer. Finally, she said, "A stranger in a red coat breaks into your house and leaves toys and puts walnuts and candy in your socks."

"Oh. I guess we don't have Christmas here because we don't wear socks."

"It's hard to put candy in a horseshoe," said Regan solemnly, and Chicory giggled, and everything was normal again, at least for a while.

Then, on the horizon, the shape of the Fair appeared. The tops of the tents were first, striped in bright colors and bedecked with flags and banners. They grew taller as the herd approached, looming more than twice the height of the tallest centaurs, and the structures around them began to materialize. There were smaller tents, wooden constructs that looked somewhere between temporary and permanent, and there were *people*. Centaurs like the ones Regan knew. More delicate centaurs with the lower bodies of graceful deer and the spreading antlers to match. Satyrs and fauns and minotaurs and bipeds with human torsos but equine legs and haunches, like centaurs that had been clipped neatly in half. It was a wider variety of hooved humanity than Regan could have imagined. She sat up straighter, gripping Chicory's waist, and stared.

The herd continued at the same pace, neither slowing nor speeding up. When they reached the wide woven archway marking the entrance to the Fair, Pansy waved them to a stop and turned her attention on the girls. "Be careful," she said in a low tone. "Don't start anything you're not certain you'll be able to finish. Chicory, if anyone makes a grab for Regan, you run."

Chicory nodded, suddenly solemn. Regan tightened her grip around the centaur girl's waist, holding on as if she feared someone was going to snatch her off at any moment. Pansy nodded, face splitting in a wide grin.

"All right, kids, go and have fun!" she said. "The Fair belongs to you today!" She leaned over and slapped Chicory on the flank, startling the girl into leaping forward, crossing the boundary line into the Fair itself.

The whispers and pointing started immediately, as everyone who saw them stopped to stare at Regan. Some of them looked startled, some amazed, and a small few looked almost enraged, like they were looking at something obscene. One of the deer-centaurs started to cry, clapping her hands over her mouth.

"They're just not used to how ugly you are yet," said Chicory. "Once they get used to looking at your weird face, they won't stare like that."

Regan snorted, discomfort melting away in the face of familiar teasing. "You better be nice to me, or I won't help you with your hooves anymore."

"Will so."

"Why?"

"Because you love me too much to let me split my hooves when you don't have to." Chicory trotted on, angling toward the delicious smells filling the air. "We can get roast nuts and baked apples and fish pies in the market square. Real good food, not that mush Rose and Daisy like to serve."

Regan, who would have been willing to commit crimes for Oreos, made a noncommittal noise. Chicory laughed and kept going, ignoring the murmurs of the crowd behind them, some of whom had started to move closer before she started moving away.

"Why are they so surprised?" asked Regan. "None of you were this surprised."

"Oh, we were. We just knew better than to show it. Pansy found you because you were meant to be with us—humans always wind up where they're supposed to be, and that made you ours. And we didn't want to scare you off. Even I know how important it is for a herd to have the honor of hosting a human. We'll be remembered for centuries after you do whatever it is you've come here to do. You'll save the Queen or change the world, and our descendants will be honored for things they had nothing to do with. I know the aunts are going courting, and it's because you're here."

"Me? I thought it was because your mother said you needed a playmate."

Chicory snorted. "It takes a year to have a foal, and they're useless when they're born. Even worse than unicorn babies. I won't play with anyone who comes out of this courtship for a long, long time. Mama didn't want another foal until I was old enough to work with the rest of the herd, and no one else could afford to go courting. Our flock does pretty well, but not *that* well."

Regan was starting to realize that even what little she'd thought she understood about centaur relationships was wrong. She shook her head, trying to find the words she needed to unsnarl a confusing knot that was only getting worse the longer she let it stay tied. Finally, in a strangled voice, she asked, "They're paying for boyfriends?"

"Is a boyfriend like a husband?"

"Yes."

"Then yes."

"But that's . . ."

"How else is the stallion supposed to know the foals will be cared for? You have to show you can support the baby you're hoping to have before you can go about getting one. And since it's the mare who walks away with the foal, it's only fair the stallion should get something out of the deal.

So Mama and the aunts and anyone else interested in court-ing go to see the stallions, and some of them will come back with foals, and some won't."

"But . . ." It was a reasonable arrangement. Regan could see that. It certainly would have simplified things for most of the high school students she'd known, who seemed to be constantly preoccupied by the question of who was dating who, or who wanted to be dating who, or who had a crush on who. Laurel had been starting that, and so had some of the other girls, in the months before Regan ran away. She'd never quite seen the point. When compared to spending her time playing, boys were just sort of . . . boring.

Regan stopped, composing her thoughts, before she said, "Where I come from, 'husband' means you're only ever with your wife. Husbands and wives live together, and raise chil-dren together, and try to be happy. My father says a good marriage takes work, usually after Mom asks him to catch a big spider and take it outside for her."

"Husbands sometimes have more than one wife, but never more than two or three," said Chicory. "If they sire a colt, they have to be prepared to take him on as their own, and too many wives would make that hard."

Regan blinked slowly. "This is really complicated."

"I bet husbands are complicated where you come from, too. You just aren't old enough to know all the ways how." Chicory cantered to a stop in front of a line of small, brightly colored wagons. They weren't big enough to have housed an adult centaur; instead, satyrs and fauns and more of those odd horse-legged people leaned out of their serving windows, handing bags and bowls of their wares to waiting customers. "I want baked apples."

Regan inhaled, taking her time about it, letting the mingled aromas of a dozen types of unfamiliar treat fill her nose. Then she slid off Chicory's back, steadying herself on the other girl's side as she waited for the feeling to come back into her thighs, and said, "I want some of those roast nuts, and a fish pie. I have money."

Chicory pawed at the ground, clearly uncertain. "I'll come with you."

"No one's going to snatch me in the *food court*," said Regan, the uneasy awareness that children had been snatched in food courts before flooding in on the heels of her words. But that was in another world, one filled with bullying, backstabbing humans, not in this brighter, cleaner world of horse-people and honest answers. She would be fine here.

"Okay," Chicory said. "But we don't leave the wagons, right? You'll get your lunch and I'll get mine, and then we'll sit together to eat it." There was a cluster of low wooden tables off to one side, about half with benches, presumably for the satyrs and other bipeds to use.

"We don't leave," Regan agreed, smiling broadly as Chicory backed up and turned away, heading for the wagon that was distributing apples.

Feeling freer, even though her friend was only a few feet away, Regan took a deep breath and approached the nearest wagon, where a faun was passing out bags of roast nuts that smelled like absolute heaven. She stopped when she reached the window, smiling at the woman with the delicate deer's antlers growing from her temples.

"One bag of nuts, please," she said in her sweetest talking-to-adults tone.

"That will be one bale," said the faun as she reached back and grabbed a bag. Then she gasped, eyes going wide. "You're the human!" she exclaimed. "I'm so sorry, I didn't realize, you looked like a silene—"

"What's a silene?" asked Regan, removing the money bag from her belt and holding it up. She hoped the faun's obvious awe would keep her from taking advantage of Regan's equally obvious ignorance. "I'm sorry, I don't know which one's a bale. Can you pick it out for me, please?"

"Of course. I'm so sorry." The faun pushed the bag of nuts into Regan's hand and took the coin purse, opening it and picking through until she found a mid-sized, goldish coin. She held it up for Regan to see. "This is a bale. The silver ones are sheafs, and the copper ones are grains. Ten grains to the sheaf, five sheafs to the bale."

If that was the exchange system, these were very expensive nuts. Regan silently vowed to enjoy them as much as she could, even as she nodded and reached for her coin purse. "Thank you," she said politely. "I heard there was someone selling fish pies? Can you tell me where they are?"

The faun looked briefly reluctant, although whether it was at the idea of returning the money or the idea of sending Regan away, Regan couldn't have said. Finally, she passed the purse back, leaned out the window, and pointed to the left. "Blue wagon, two down. You asked what a silene was?

Well, it's a silene who'll sell you your pie, human. Thank you for bringing your business to my unworthy stall."

Regan took a step back, tying the coin pouch back to her waistband where it belonged, and began walking briskly in the direction of the blue wagon. Inside, one of the horse-legged people she'd seen before was lining up small single-serving pies on a tray. She stopped a few feet away, not wanting to startle him the way she'd startled the faun.

He glanced up, and nearly dropped the pie he was holding. "Human!" he exclaimed, almost accusatorially.

"Yes," said Regan. "I'm here to buy a pie, please."

"You came all the way to the Fair just to buy a pie?" His ears were like a horse's as well. They twitched as he stared at her, the pie in his hand apparently forgotten.

"No," she said. "I've been traveling with one of the unicorn-tending herds, and we're here to sell the excess unicorns to the livestock traders before winter. But I came to the food court because my friend Chicory mentioned pies." There was Chicory trotting languidly toward her, a baked apple on a stick in either hand. "Please, can I buy one of your pies?" This was getting frustrating. She hadn't realized how normally her herd treated her until she was faced with people who didn't treat her the same way.

The vendor seemed to snap out of his amazement, and thrust the pie he was holding across the counter at her. "Here you are," he said. "I hope you'll enjoy it."

"How much, please?"

"Nothing. For a human in the Hooflands, nothing." He flapped his hands when she tried to argue. "Anyone who sees you eating my pie will want one of their own, and I'll make so much money from being able to say you bought it here that there's no sense in charging you. You're doing me a favor by taking that pie."

"Um," said Regan, uncertain. "If you're sure."

"I'm sure! A human, eating my pie. The world is full of wonders." The silene smiled broadly, exposing incisors wider and flatter than her own. Regan smiled hesitantly back and turned toward Chicory, intending to walk over to her friend.

The bag jerked down over her head cut off her view before she could move. Someone grabbed her around the waist, yanking her off her feet, and she had time for one despairing cry as her untasted food tumbled out of her hands and she was toted unceremoniously away.

In the distance, she could hear Chicory screaming. She drew in a breath to scream, too, only for something to strike her in the back of the head, hard enough to turn the world white with pain. The darkness rose up to claim her, and the darkness was all.

PART III

THE CONSEQUENCES OF
BEING HUMAN

10 TAKEN

REGAN WOKE WITH AN aching skull and hair that felt sticky, like something had been spilled on the back of her head. *Blood*. No other explanation made sense. Also, she was on her side in a bed of hay in a dark room, her hands in front of her, her wrists and ankles tied together with some sort of twine. She tried to sit up, only to topple over when she failed to find the balance she needed to remain upright.

There were voices in the distance. She went still, straining to hear what they were saying.

"—centaurs are going to kill us," said one of them, unfamiliar, deep and rumbling, like rocks rolling across the bottom of the sea.

"Only if they catch us before we hand the brat over," said another, lighter and higher, but still unfamiliar. "Did you have to hit her so hard?"

"The little filly was going to catch up to us if the human had the freedom to fight," said the first voice. "I did what I had to do. The Queen's guard will pay dearly for delivery of the creature, dead or alive. Dead might even be better. Dead doesn't overthrow the government."

"She's just a child," said a third voice. This one Regan recognized, and she stiffened with the indignity of it all. It was the faun who'd sold her the bag of nuts, the one who'd been willing to take her money. She must have signaled the others as soon as Regan had walked away. How dare she? How *dare* she?

Regan began to squirm, trying to loosen the knots around her ankles. She didn't need her hands to run, and she was more likely to hurt herself if she rubbed twine against bare skin. So she kicked as much as she could, and was still kicking when a door suddenly opened and spilled light into the room. She froze, wide-eyed, and stared at the slim figure silhouetted in the opening, antlers visible to either side of her head. It was the faun.

"You're awake," she said. "I'm sorry we had to hit you. That wasn't part of the plan."

"So untie me and let me hit you back," said Regan.

"You know I can't do that," said the faun.

Regan narrowed her eyes. "But you can hand me over to people who want to hurt me," she accused.

The faun took another step into the room, hooves clacking delicately against the floor. "No one wants to hurt you," she said, with what sounded like genuine surprise and regret in her tone. "But you're worth so much money that it would be irresponsible of us to let you go wandering around free, the way those centaur savages you've been with did. The Queen will take excellent care of you."

Regan stared at her, heart suddenly beating too hard and lungs suddenly tight, unable to take in any additional air. Finally, she managed to wheeze, "The Q-Queen?"

"Yes. Doesn't every colt and filly dream of meeting Her Sunlit Majesty?" The faun's tone was artificially sweet, the voice of someone who didn't care for children trying to empathize with one. "Queen Kagami has everything you could ever dream of wanting. A palace, servants, the finest food—nothing like what you've been experiencing with those savages."

Regan, who had experienced love, and care, and acceptance with the centaurs, said nothing at all.

The faun seemed to take her silence for awe, because she took another delicate step toward Regan. "They should have taken you to her right away, so you could begin fulfilling your destiny."

"I don't believe in destiny."

"Destiny believes in you." The fawn took a breath. "I really am sorry we had to hit you."

"I'm sorry too," said Regan.

"You understand this was for your own good."

"I understand you think this was for my own good." Regan shifted in the straw, pulling herself as far back as she could manage with the twine binding her ankles. "I understand you think you know what's best for me, when you've never met me before and don't know what *I* want."

"There's nothing personal about it," said the faun. "Humans must be taken to the Queen, and if we're the ones to deliver you, we'll get paid. So much money that our families will be safe and protected for years to come. You'll be pampered and cosseted and cared for. Surely a little slice of your freedom is a fair price to pay for knowing our families will never go to bed hungry."

Regan had never met the faun's family, and while she was a generally kind and generous child, she was still a child; this wasn't an argument that would gain any ground with her. She glared and shook her head. "What about *my* family?" she asked. "They took care of me. Shouldn't they be rewarded for that, if anyone is? And if I just disappear, they won't know what happened! They'll look for me forever."

"You're the only human in the world. You don't have a family."

"I have the herd."

"They're not your family, and if you think they'll keep looking for you once the season turns and the snow comes down, you don't know them as well as you think you do. Centaurs are barely more than beasts." The faun shook her head, ears flattening in disgust. "They'll never be loyal to you. They'll never come looking."

"They took care of me when they didn't have to," snarled Regan, and kicked her feet again, straining against the twine. "They're my friends, and they're as good as my family, and they'll come for me. They'll find me, and you'll be sorry."

"Be still, child," said the faun, sounding concerned.

"I won't!" said Regan, kicking harder. The twine felt like it was starting to give. She might be able to break free soon if she kept this up.

She was less sure of what would happen after that, but anything would be better than being tied up and helpless.

"Hush!" said the faun, casting an anxious glance over her shoulder at the door she'd entered through. "You don't want to—"

"What's going on in there?" boomed the unfamiliar voice Regan had heard before. She stopped kicking and shrank back in the straw, trying to make herself as small as she could. Whoever that voice belonged to, they didn't sound happy.

The clomping of massive hooves echoed down the hall. The door was pushed wider open, and one of the bull-headed men she'd seen at the fair ducked through, horns barely clearing the frame. Seen this close, he was terrifying, a mountain of a man walking through a world built to a much smaller scale. Each of his hooves was larger than her entire face. He swung his muzzle around to face her, expression bovine and unreadable, and snorted.

"You making trouble back here, *human*?" he demanded.

Irritation won out over fear. "How could I?" she asked. "I'm tied up and my head hurts, because you hit me! I didn't do anything to you!"

"You exist," he replied. "Humans only ever mean upheaval. You wouldn't be here if you weren't coming to make trouble. The Queen wants you where she can keep an eye on you, and I'm happy to be the one to deliver you."

"I'm not a package, I'm a person!"

"You're a human. Whether you're a person is still up for

debate. Now be quiet, or I'll give the Queen your corpse and tell her it couldn't be helped. If the universe really wants us to have a human, it'll send another one. The hills are heavy with the bones of would-be heroes." He jerked his massive head toward the faun. "Come on. We're ready to leave." Then he strode out of the room, leaving the faun to anxiously follow after him, glancing over her shoulder at Regan. In moments, Regan was alone again.

She lay on her side in the straw, shaking with a combination of fear and fury that put her teeth on edge and made her feel as if every nerve in her body was on fire. She wanted to scream. She wanted to rage until they returned to silence her, and then she would kick and bite and do everything else she could to make them regret taking her from the Fair.

And then they would kill her, and she would never see her family—either family—again. No. Rage was the wrong answer, at least right now. She forced herself to breathe slowly in and out, and began twisting her ankles again. The bull-headed man had hooves. All of them had hooves. None of them had any experience with human-type legs, so maybe they hadn't tied her up the right way, and she could get loose.

She didn't know how long she'd been there, twisting and straining, when she heard a small snapping sound and her ankles came abruptly apart. She rolled onto her back, letting her legs fall where they would, and waited for the tingling in her feet to fade. Once that was done, she squirmed further around to lever herself onto her knees and from there to her feet.

Regan squinted against the dimness, trying to figure out

what was supposed to happen next. She was alone in a dark room with no weapons, no allies, and no use of her hands. But she had her legs, and they'd done their best to take those away from her, which meant they were worried she'd escape. She knew where her kidnappers were, behind the one door she was sure of, and so she tiptoed in the other direction, becoming aware of another advantage in the process.

Everyone in the Hooflands had hooves. They never walked quietly, unless it was on grass or soft earth, and while there was a layer of straw covering the floor, it wasn't enough to muffle the sound of hoofbeats. Human feet in sneakers worn smooth as river rocks were another matter. She moved silently across the room, and no one came to see what she was doing, or seemed to realize she was loose.

It was too dark for Regan to see anything, so she placed her joined hands against the wall at roughly the height of a knob or latch and began tiptoeing around the edge of the room, waiting for the moment when her fingers would snag against something that didn't fit.

She had made it almost halfway around when she felt cool metal, not machined like the latches back at home, but beaten against an anvil until it turned smooth. It was textured, something like brick and something like rough wood and something like a wrought iron fence. Regan swallowed, closing her eyes in silent hope, before grabbing it and pushing down as hard as she could.

If she'd been a smaller or less athletic child, she might not have had the strength to move the latch. She leaned against it with everything she had, and it clicked, a tiny but somehow terrifying sound, before it swung away from her, taking a large piece of wall with it.

Outside, it was dark, and the moonlight hung silvery over an unfamiliar field. She took a shaking step forward, and then another, until she was standing next to the building where she'd been confined, and could see that it was closer to a traditional barn than anything else she'd seen in the Hooflands. It was more constructed-looking than the long-houses the centaurs favored, with a sloping roof and white-washed walls.

She took another step, and then she was running, racing for the distant line of what she assumed was a fence. Every time her feet hit the ground, it sent a jarring impact all the way along her spine to the sore spot on her skull, which throbbed and ached in tempo with her flight. She didn't slow down. Instead, she ran faster, loping along until she felt like she could outrun Chicory, like she was the fastest thing in the world.

Behind her, she heard a door slam open and the bull-headed man's angry bellow as he realized his prey was escaping. If he'd been a centaur, it would have already been over, with no chance of escape, but he was a biped like her, only bigger and bulkier, which meant he might be slower. The faun and the silene were smaller, sure, but they had less motivation to run than she did; she was confident enough to keep on going. The throbbing in her head got worse and worse, and her lungs began to ache, but she had to get away.

Destiny wasn't real. Destiny was for people like Laurel, who could pin everything they had to an idea that the world was supposed to work in a certain way, and refuse to let it change. If these people said her destiny was to see the Queen, she would prove them wrong. She wasn't their chosen one. She was just Regan, and as Regan, she ran.

Then the fence was there. She couldn't climb it with her hands tied, so she dropped to the ground and rolled below the bottom bar. For once, her delayed puberty seemed like a blessing and not a punishment; if she'd developed the hips or breasts she'd been envying on the other girls before coming to the Hooflands, she might not have been able to fit.

Unfortunately, rolling meant she saw what was behind her, and what was behind her was the faun, running faster than seemed possible with her narrow legs and cloven hooves. Regan rolled, moving out of reach just as the faun reached the fence. She lunged across it, trying to grab the human girl, but Regan was already scrambling to her feet and back-pedaling across the grass, getting further out of range. The faun began climbing the fence, and the other two were close behind her, their hooves not carrying them as quickly. They carried them all the same.

Regan spun around and broke back into a run, heading for the distant smudge of a tree line. There would be kelpies there if there was water, and perytons if there wasn't, and either way, she'd be delivering herself into their terrible teeth—but their teeth seemed suddenly less dangerous than the people chasing her. Their teeth didn't want to bind her to a destiny.

She was halfway to the trees when a dark shape loomed out of the underbrush, racing toward her at a pace she couldn't have hoped to match, much less beat. *I guess the kelpies heard me coming*, she thought, already resigned to what was going to happen next. Still she kept running, as hard and as fast as she could, until it felt like the muscles in her thighs would tear and break away, until it felt like there was nothing in the world but running. At least she'd die knowing she'd tried; at least she'd go down fighting to the last to survive.

Then the figure drew close enough for her to see the moonlight glinting off the steel-gray of her coat and the matching steel-gray of her hair, and Regan's heart leapt as she held tied hands out to Pansy, silently pleading. The centaur barely slowed as she reached down, grabbed Regan around the waist, and slung the girl across her back like a sack of wheat, wheeling and running back the way she'd come.

Regan watched as the figures of her kidnappers dwindled in the distance and were gone.

11 THE AFTERMATH OF THE UNTHINKABLE

PANSY RAN WHAT FELT like forever but was probably no more than a mile before she cantered to a stop, twisted around, and scooped Regan off her back, setting the girl on her feet.

"Give me your hands," she said, producing a knife from inside her vest. "I'll cut that twine." Her eyes searched Regan's face, concern and fear evident. "Did they hurt you?"

"They hit me in the head when they took me," said Regan, obediently sticking her hands out. "It still hurts. But I'm not dizzy or anything, and my dad always said that was how you could tell if someone had a concussion." A sudden wave of almost painful homesickness washed over her. She missed her parents. She missed her home. She missed her *horses*. They must be so confused about why she stopped coming to the stable. They must miss her so much.

"Oh, honey, I'm sorry," said Pansy, gently taking her wrists and slicing through the twine with a flick of her knife. Pain followed immediately after, rushing into the grooves the twine had cut into her skin, and Regan made a soft sound as she pulled her hands away and began rubbing her wrists. "We should never have let you and Chicory go off alone the way we did. I guess we were thinking the Fair would be safe for you the way it's always been for us. We should have known better. That's our fault."

"Chicory." Regan's eyes widened. "Is Chicory okay?"

"She will be, now that we have you back. Poor girl's been eating herself alive out of the fear that we'd never see you again and it would be all her fault, or she was, when I left to try tracking you down." Pansy shook her head. "She's just a foal. We treat her like she's almost grown because we don't know what else to do with her, but she shouldn't be asked to take things this heavy onto her shoulders before she's old enough to pull a plow."

"People keep asking me to save the world." Regan couldn't keep the bitterness out of her tone.

"Yes," said Pansy. "That's what humans do. But the Queen will see that you're still a child, so I'm sure she won't ask you to do anything dangerous. Maybe someday, but not now."

"The Queen thinks I'm going to do something to hurt her."

Pansy became abruptly very still. "What do you mean?"

"The people who grabbed me said it was because Queen Kagami told them to. They were going to take me to her. They said . . ." She swallowed, hard. "They said she wouldn't care if I was alive or dead when they got there. I think they were going to kill me if I made too much trouble."

"They said the *Queen* told them to take you." Pansy's

expression, already grim, darkened further, becoming sepulchral. She offered her arm. "Come. We need to get back to the herd. Chicory will be so relieved to see that you're safe."

Regan took the arm without argument, swinging herself onto Pansy's back and wrapping her own arms around Pansy's waist. As soon as her hands were joined, Pansy broke into a gallop, hooves churning at the earth, hair whipping out behind her to slap Regan in the face. She held on tighter, feeling a traitorous rush of joy run along her spine. This was what she loved. Riding, running, the world rushing by like a chalk drawing, smudged and blurred and beautiful.

In all too short a time, Pansy was trotting to a stop in front of a longhouse—not one of the ones Regan had seen before. The unicorns were scattered around the field out front, cropping at the grass, ears swiveling as they listened for danger. A few of them lifted their heads as Regan slid down from Pansy's back. Most didn't even bother.

They proceeded inside, where the rest of the herd was waiting. Chicory had a black eye and one arm was bound in a sling. She turned toward the sound of the door opening, straightened, and cried, "Regan!" before rushing to them, shoving past her aunts in the process. She flung her good arm around Regan's shoulders, buried her face against the other girl's neck, and started to sob.

"I'm okay, Chicory, I'm okay," said Regan, awkwardly patting her on the back. "Just be careful with my head, please. It hurts."

Chicory let her go as fast as if she'd suddenly admitted to having fleas. Regan stood awkwardly as the rest of the herd clustered around. Pansy put her hands on Regan's shoulders, holding her where she was.

"How did you find me?" Regan asked, craning her neck around to look at Pansy.

"Only one road out of the Fair from the merchant stalls," said Pansy gruffly. "There's always a lot of shouting during setup, with everyone trying to come in at once. They had to pull a whole food wagon out of the rotation during the Fair proper, and that's strange enough that it gave me a place to start looking. I've been following you almost since you were taken."

"Oh," said Regan, not feeling as relieved as she wanted to. She'd still been in danger. Pansy had been right behind them, but they could have killed her before she was recovered, and she'd have to live with that knowledge forever.

Pansy shifted her attention from Regan to the rest of the herd. "The kidnappers were in the service of Queen Kagami," she said.

"They said they were going to get a lot of money for taking me to her," said Regan. "Dead or alive."

The other centaurs recoiled, all save for Daisy, who was the oldest among them, and the most difficult to shock. She pushed her way forward, stopping next to Chicory. "We don't doubt you, child, but are you sure they weren't lying about the Queen asking them to take you?"

"I don't know," said Regan. "But they thought I was asleep when they said the part about getting a reward for me dead."

Daisy looked gravely at the others. "Then you know what must be done."

Pansy nodded. "I do."

Regan looked between them. "I don't!" she said. "What are you going to do?"

"We're going to run, child," said Daisy. "We leave the flock, and we run, as far as our hooves will carry us. You are the future of the Hooflands. It is your destiny. The doors open only when we're standing on the cusp of greatest need, and you wouldn't be here if they hadn't chosen you. That the Queen would set herself against you is regrettable, and a sign, perhaps, that she has forgotten the balance of things."

"What does the Queen *do*, anyway?" asked Regan, trying not to resent the fact that even the centaurs thought she was here to fulfill some unwanted destiny. She wouldn't. She couldn't. She refused. "She rules, but what does that mean?"

"She sets the prices for herds and harvest," said Daisy. "She decides which livestock will have value and which will not. She sets guards against the deep forest where perytons and kelpies live, to keep us safe. Her armies watch the borders against invasion from outside."

"Wait," said Regan, who had never heard a murmur of anything outside the Hooflands. "What lives outside the Hooflands? And what invasion?"

Daisy looked uncomfortable. "No one knows," she said. "There hasn't been one in living memory. But the Queen keeps us safe. She walks in sunlight, blessed and kept by the

Hooflands themselves, and without her, we would fall to darkness."

"But the price for our livestock has been going down as long as I've been old enough to know the herd's finances, and the price of other food keeps going up," said Chicory. "Is she really keeping us safe if we have to keep working harder in order not to starve?"

"I don't know," said Daisy. "She's the Queen. That means we follow and obey her. Or it always has, before she became a danger to our Regan. She's our Queen. Regardless, if there are sides to choose, we've already chosen ours." She knelt, resting her weight on her forelegs while her hind remained straight and high, tail lashing. "We have always held the land above the one who rules it."

Regan stared, shocked and a little terrified, as one by one, the centaurs who had become her family mirrored Daisy's gesture. Finally, she turned to Pansy and asked, "What will happen to the unicorns?"

Pansy smiled. "There are other herders. We speak with them often. Several know what happened, that you were taken from the Fair. When we haven't come to speak with them for several days, they'll send someone to check on us. Finding us gone and the flock alone, they'll do what good caretakers always do, and they'll care for them. We'll have to buy new stock when this is over, but that's a small price to pay for the survival of our world and the safety of our child."

She reached out then, gently brushing Regan's hair away from her face with one thick-nailed hand.

"You ready to run away with us, kiddo?"

Unable to speak past the lump in her throat, Regan nodded.

Later, neither she nor Chicory would be able to remember many details about that night. There was a brief squabble over who she was going to ride with, before Aster said Chicory's legs were fine, even if her arm was broken, and Regan could ride with her. The rest of the herd would be carrying their possessions. They were leaving the unicorns, but taking their resources—clothing, food, tools, and Daisy's stores of herbs and tinctures. They were going to disappear, not die. That meant taking some precautions.

"The Queen's castle is south of here," said Daisy. "We go north."

The others agreed, and when they were done packing and strapping their worldly goods to one another's backs, Pansy lifted Regan off her feet and set her gently astride Chicory. Mindful of her friend's injuries, Regan slid her arms around her waist and held on tight as Chicory set off at a gentle trot, following the adults.

They moved down the road in as close to silence as eight adult centaurs and one filly could manage, leaving the longhouse and unicorns behind. Rose was the last out of the yard; she looked sadly at the unicorns as she closed the gate behind herself, locking them inside. Then she trotted after the others, catching up in short order.

They walked through the night and all the way to morning. Regan fell asleep on Chicory's back, resting her weight on the other girl's shoulders. When the sunlight shining in her eyes finally woke her, she opened them on what seemed to be a whole new world.

Gone were the cultivated fields and grazing herds she'd grown accustomed to, replaced by orchards and thorn briars and the looming outline of a massive forest. There were no fences or walls, only the stretch of the land in all directions, stopped to the north by a line of mountains the color of slate, topped with snow and seemingly taller than the sky. What looked like a rabbit with a deer's antlers dashed out of the brush and across the path, vanishing into the tall grass.

The path was another change. It was pressed dirt, studded with wildflowers and weeds, and nowhere near straight or regular enough to earn the title of "road." Pansy looked over, smiling wearily.

"Good, you're awake," she said. "We'll keep going until nightfall, but where we're headed is somewhere no one will think to look for us. You'll be safe."

"Where are we?" asked Regan muzzily. She rubbed her eyes, sitting up straighter.

"The northern edge of the Hooflands," said Pansy. "We won't go past the border, but we'll go deep into the forest."

"It's seen as too dangerous for outsiders," said Aster. "That's why it's the last place the Queen's spies would think to look for us, but my sisters and I grew up here. The people of the forest tend to keep to themselves, and the perytons aren't as big of a threat as people make them out to be. We'll be fine, as long as we can find shelter. The herds here don't keep animals like we do in the south, so there are no longhouses, but we can keep our eyes open for a traveler's cottage. If there's no one already there, we can stay until we build something more permanent."

It was all so much, and it bordered on dizzying. Regan gestured to the briars around them, heavy with purple-red berries. "Are those edible?" she asked. They looked like someone had successfully crossed blackberries with raspberries, and she liked both those fruits well enough.

Aster nodded. "They are, and good for you as well."

"Good." Regan leaned over, filling her hands with berries as Chicory continued to walk, keeping pace with the adults as best as she could. The berries were sweet and tart at the same time, and they soothed Regan's thirst even as they filled her stomach.

So it was that the herd came to the north.

It would have been easier on them if those who had gone courting at the Fair hadn't found husbands before Regan was taken, but the world has never traded in "easy" when it didn't have to. Rose, Lily, and Bramble soon learned they were with foal, and while they fussed about not being able to go back to the Fair if they had colts instead of fillies, they were all pleased by the situation. The "traveler's cottage" Aster had mentioned turned out to be a barn-like building at the edge of the wood. There was room inside for all of them, but there wouldn't be once the babies came. There was also a chance other travelers would know it was there, and Regan's presence meant they needed someplace better concealed. They slept there for three nights while Clover and Aster walked the forest, looking for a place that hadn't already been claimed.

On the morning of the fourth day, they returned with news of a clearing big enough to suit their needs, near a creek shaded by fruit trees. The herd relocated at once, and construction began the next day.

Pansy put her tools to good use, felling trees with a combination of sawing and well-placed kicks, then helping the others plane those trees down into usable planks. Chicory and Regan couldn't participate, the one due to her broken arm and the other due to her size, but they were able to forage for food and stand watch. When things began coming together, it happened very quickly.

"It's like a barn-raising," said Regan, watching the walls rise into view as the adults pulled them off the ground.

"What's a barn?" asked Chicory.

Regan laughed and hugged her.

This was a new place, well hidden from the danger posed by a Queen she'd never met, and far from the doors. They couldn't find her here, she was sure of that. The fact that this meant she couldn't go home never crossed her mind. In her relief at evading her kidnappers and slipping away from the Queen, she allowed herself to relax.

It took four days for the new "cottage" to be habitable. The interior was one large room, with individual stalls carved out of the back half of the space. Pansy and Aster spent an afternoon building a long table like the ones they'd had back in the longhouses, and once it was positioned at the center of the cottage, the previously impersonal space began to feel like home. Chicory and Regan stayed close, mindful of the dangers they had been warned roamed the woods. Perytons might be less aggressive than kelpies, but Regan had no interest in being eaten.

Finally, on the evening of the fourth day, Pansy called them to come inside, and they did, stepping into a warm, well-lit space that smelled of sap and sawdust and the heat coming off the bodies of the adults. The table was already set for dinner, with all the fruits of the forest laid out and waiting to be enjoyed.

Regan smiled, looking around at her family, and decided, in that moment, that she was home; she never wanted to leave, ever again.

12 TIME DOES AS TIME WILL

"CHICORY!" ASTER PLANTED HER hands on her hips and threw her head back to make her voice carry further. "You need to come back here *right now,* young lady!"

"Aw, Mom." Chicory cantered out of the forest, a bow in her hand and a pheasant slung over her shoulder, feathers fanning down her back like a cloak. "Why do you need me now?"

"The babies won't stop crying, and Lily's at her wit's end." All three women had foaled, two colts and a filly. They were old enough now to have opinions about things, and those opinions tended to feed into one another, so that a single cranky baby could result in three sets of healthy screams.

Regan spent as little time as possible inside the cottage, citing her sensitive human hearing as the reason for her absence. Only Daisy seemed to realize she was lying. Regan's ears were no more sensitive than a centaur's, and now that she'd adjusted to the volume at which they lived their lives, she shouted as loudly as the rest of them. Daisy smirked whenever Regan pled her way out of a situation due to her hearing, and let her run off thinking she'd fooled the adults.

Chicory wasn't so lucky. As the youngest member of the herd, the logic the adults lived by seemed to think she would be the best at caring for young things, since she remembered what it was to be one of them. She found herself tapped for babysitting any time the adults got tired of it, which was often. It didn't help that none of them had any experience with boys or brothers, not even the three sisters who had come from the north in the first place. These boys were the sons of fathers they might never see, not while they needed to keep Regan hidden and safe.

So Chicory found herself caring for a small horde of shrieking hellions who inadvertently answered many of Regan's questions about centaur development, questions that had always felt too intrusive and potentially insulting. Like horses, they'd been born capable of supporting their own heads, already prepared to wobble around the cottage on shaky legs with knobbly knees. They had started at what looked to Regan like roughly two years of age, but with the dexterity and naivete of human infants, and they had remained almost exactly the same size for the two years that followed, as their brains caught up to their bodies.

The same couldn't be said for Chicory and Regan. Both shot up, gaining height at a speed that had rendered Regan's original clothes unwearable before the end of that first winter. She remained slender as a reed, arms and legs ropy with muscle, chest as flat as ever. Chicory, on the other hand, grew in other directions as well, necessitating a new kind of vest to keep her breasts from impeding her when she ran through the forest. Regan found herself needing to be much more careful where she put her hands when she rode. Not that she needed to hold on all that often anymore; they moved as one creature when they ran together, and Regan learned to mount by dropping out of the trees directly onto Chicory's back.

Regan's ability to climb was a constant mysterious delight to the little ones, whose hooves didn't grant them anywhere near her dexterity. Even Chicory was sometimes surprised to look up and realize how high Regan had gone. The adult centaurs exchanged knowing looks and watched her go, their human, growing and learning in safety, well outside the reach of the Queen. Their loyalties had shifted forever on that long-ago day at the Fair, when the Queen to whom they had previously pledged themselves had allied herself with those who would harm the girl most of them thought of almost as a daughter.

Five years passed in the shadow of the trees, the foundations of their cottage sinking deeper into the soil, taking stability from the passage of time. The colts began growing again when they were almost four years old, putting on height at an incredible rate, vocabularies expanding by the day. Chicory began to enjoy babysitting duties. Regan learned to climb all the way to the tops of the trees, the better to escape her tiny herd of unwanted admirers. Daisy threatened to tie a rope around her ankle so she could be hauled back down when it was time for lessons. Life went on.

The perytons who lived in the deep part of the forest

resembled nothing so much as winged deer that had been skinned but somehow managed to keep walking around under their own power. They were carnivores, their powerful jaws making short work of any squirrels or rabbits that came too close. They snapped at Regan when she approached, but didn't flee. They didn't press their attacks, either. She began following them through the woods, making an effort to get as close as she could without losing a finger, and was able to track them to the burrows where they lived and raised their young, gangly, half-fledged things that tore and snarled at each other, learning to hunt one mock-battle at a time. Pansy scolded her, telling her to leave the terrible things alone, but Regan was enchanted and no longer accustomed to being told "no."

"You keep telling me I'm supposed to save the world," she said, after one particularly intense scolding. "How can I do that if I run away from a stupid skinless deer?"

Pansy folded her arms. "You keep saying you don't believe in destiny. This was easier before you decided to grow up," she said. "Can't you be a little girl again? I liked that better."

Regan laughed. Here, surrounded by people who loved her but had no idea what humans were supposed to be like, she was normal. No one seemed to notice or care that puberty was passing her almost entirely by, and somehow, that took any potential sting out of the situation. So she wasn't changing the way Chicory was. She wasn't the same as Chicory, didn't have hooves or a tail or pointed ears. Wishing to be a centaur wouldn't change anything about who she was, and so there was no point in wishing for anything else about herself to change.

"No," she said. "But I'll always be yours." She hugged Pansy then, the top of her head coming up to the centaur's collarbone, before letting go and running off into the woods.

Her days were split between running wild and working with Daisy, who insisted her education mattered more than anything. The colts were accident-prone; she had already splinted several arms and stitched up several gashes too deep to leave to heal on their own. She knew every medicinal herb that grew in the woods, and several that didn't, although she wasn't sure she'd recognize them if she saw them growing fresh, having learnt their shapes and properties from the dried specimens in Daisy's saddlebags. It was a long, slow apprenticeship, and she sometimes worried that as the colts aged, one of them would show an interest, and Daisy would abandon her in favor of a member of her own kind. Daisy showed no signs of doing so, and Regan began to relax. Her ability to climb let her bring back rare herbs for Daisy to dry and add to the stocks, gathered from the tops of trees and the bottoms of gullies.

And time marched on.

It had been more than five years since Regan ran away from school on purpose and ran away from home by mistake. She barely thought of her parents anymore, and always with the faintest, burning tinge of guilt, like she'd betrayed them and their love by falling in love with another world, one that seemed designed perfectly for her. Part of her was sure they'd forgotten her by now, consigning her to the scrapbooks of memory, and had another child living in her bedroom, getting ready to start classes at her school. Another part of her knew they'd be mourning her forever, unsure whether she was alive or dead, and that part was sorry for what she'd done, even though she hadn't done it on purpose. She would have gone back in the beginning if she'd been able to, but now she was fifteen and had been in the Hooflands for a third of her life, surrounded by people who loved her for who she was, who didn't think she was weird or try to shove her into boxes she'd had nothing to do with building. This was her home.

She was never leaving.

She was in the river when Chicory pushed the bushes aside and called, "Regan! Mom wants you at the cottage!"

It was ridiculous how they still called the vast, barn-like building a "cottage," but Regan's annoyance wasn't going to change the way language worked here, and it would have been rude to try. She straightened, icy water biting her thighs—hot showers were one of the few things she *did* miss from the land of her birth—and called back, "Why? I finished my lessons. I'm trying to get the mud out of my hair before it has time to dry."

Chicory shrugged. "I don't know. She just told me to go and get you, and you'd said you were going for a bath, so I knew I'd be able to find you here."

Regan glared before sinking under the water and scratching her scalp, dislodging the last chunks of mud. She surfaced and paddled toward the shore, where she had a bundle of rosemary and violets waiting. She scrubbed them against her head, hard enough to release the oils in the vegetation, then ducked under again, rinsing the flecks of smashed greenery away.

When she surfaced the second time, Chicory was on the bank, hoof scraping impatiently at the mud. "Come *on*," she said. "You know who gets in trouble if we're too slow?"

"Let me guess," said Regan. "Is it you?"

"Yes! It's me! I'm supposed to be your best friend. Getting me in trouble on purpose is mean, and friends aren't mean to each other."

Regan blinked before she smiled, slow and sweet as summer. "That's right," she said, wading to the bank and stepping out of the water. "Friends aren't mean to each other." Her clothes were folded nearby. No one in the Hooflands knew how to make a pair of trousers, which made sense, considering their anatomical differences; instead, she pulled a tunic cut for the torso of a centaur on over her head, belting it around the waist like a dress. It fell almost to her knees.

Her tunics could be bought from the traveling peddlers who sometimes came down the main road with their creaking wagons full of wonders, although the family tried to make as much for themselves as they could, to limit exposure to the outside world. Her underpants had required Rose to work out a pattern and hand-sew them from scraps of fabric. The small complications of being the only one of her kind in an entire world never failed to surprise her. Climbing onto Chicory's back, she positioned herself and said, "I'm ready when you are."

"Did you have to get up there while you were still wet?"

demanded Chicory, and broke into a trot. "I'm going to smell like wet fur all day now, thanks to you."

"Just one of the many services we offer," said Regan, and cackled with delight at her own joke.

Chicory shook her head. "Sometimes you can be so *weird*," she complained, continuing to trot toward the cottage.

Regan held on tighter. "You love me being weird."

"Do not."

"Do so! You wouldn't know what to do without me."

Chicory sobered. "You're right, I wouldn't," she said. "So when they tell you it's time to go and be a hero, I want you to tell them you can't do it."

"What?"

"Everyone says a human has to be a hero. They talk about it at night, when they think we're asleep. Mom says you're tall enough to be an adult human now, and that means you'll probably have to be a hero soon. But I don't want you to!"

"Why not?" Regan frowned. "If I came here so I could save the Hooflands, doesn't that mean I should do it? This is my home too. I don't want anything bad to happen here."

"Because humans go away after they turn into heroes!" snapped Chicory, and Regan froze. It felt like her heart had turned into a lump of ice and was sinking toward her toes, and all she could think in that moment was that toes were a horrible, *human* thing to have, and because she had them, she was going to lose this home, too. She was going to be sent somewhere else, and all because of something she'd never chosen and couldn't help.

Chicory didn't notice her distress, and continued, voice

rising with every word, "Humans come here when they get lost and the Hooflands needs saving, and they stay until it's time to save the world, and then they disappear forever!"

"Where do they go?" whispered Regan.

"No one knows," said Chicory. "Mom thinks they go back where they came from, and Aunt Bramble thinks they go to another world that has to be saved, but it doesn't matter, because they don't come *back*. Not ever."

"I will," said Regan.

"What?"

"I will. If I have to go—if there's not any way to avoid it—I'll come back. I promise. This is my home. I wish I could tell my parents I'm all right, I'm here and I'm happy and they don't need to worry about me, but I belong here. I'll come back. I'll *always* come back."

Chicory twisted to look at Regan as she continued trotting toward the cottage. "You really promise?" she asked. "You're not just saying that to make me feel better?"

"You're my best friend," said Regan. "I won't ever leave you like that."

Chicory sagged, the strange tension going out of her shoulders, and trotted to a stop in front of the cottage. "Mom's inside. She's waiting for you."

"Because that's not ominous." Regan slid off of Chicory's back, patting her reassuringly on the side, and tugged her dripping tunic into place as she walked toward the door. It was comfortingly familiar and solid. This wasn't a door that whisked human children away to new worlds. It was a door that opened to welcome them home, and was still there when they turned around. She brushed her fingertips against the wood as she stepped through, into the straw-scented gloom that always lingered under the roof.

Aster, Daisy, and Pansy were there already, waiting for her. Their expressions were serious, and Regan felt the ice gather again, chilling her from the inside out. The water dripping from her hair suddenly felt like a punishment, running down her neck and leaving clammy dread in its wake.

"There you are," said Aster in the frustrated tone she always used when Regan and Chicory ranged too far afield and needed to be brought back to heel.

"Here I am," said Regan. She turned to Daisy. Daisy, her teacher and mentor. Daisy, who would always, always tell her the truth, and wouldn't try to protect her like Pansy, or put the needs of her own daughter first, like Aster. "What's going on?" she asked in a small, pained voice. "Did I do something wrong?"

"No, child, no," said Daisy. "You did nothing wrong, or if you did"—she paused to shoot a quelling glance at the other two centaurs—"we all did. We've become too comfortable here. There aren't many centaur herds in the forest, and it's rare for them to leave, or to come back if they do. One of the traveling merchants must have grown suspicious about a new herd settling in these parts, and mentioned it where the Queen's spies could hear. She's been looking for you. She knew you were somewhere to be found, as the Hooflands have not been saved."

"And after I save the world, I disappear," said Regan, voice still small.

Pansy's head snapped up. She took a step toward Regan. "Who told you that?" she asked. "Regan, who told you that you were going to disappear?"

"Chicory did. She said you talk about it when you think we're not listening. Humans come, they save the world, and then they vanish." Regan's hands balled into fists. "I don't want to vanish. I'll still save the world if I have to, because I like it too much to let it not be saved, but I don't want to vanish."

"The Queen knows you're here," said Aster. "Her spies will *make* you disappear if we don't do something soon."

"What does she even want with me?" Regan shook her head. "It doesn't make sense. If she'd been willing to leave us alone, we'd still be in the fields with the flock, not hiding in a forest in the middle of nowhere."

"She hates you because she's what you're going to save us from," said Aster. "Things have grown worse since we left. The merchants speak of it. Prices for crops and livestock continue to drop, and the Queen sets the prices; she's to blame. The herds are starving. They can't afford to eat, to replace their tools, to go courting at the Fair—it's all falling apart. The Queen sends her soldiers to burn their fields when they refuse to tell her what she wants to know. She's no fit queen any longer. I'm sorry, but it's time for you to go to her."

"I did not agree to this," snapped Daisy. "We can hide again. There's more north in the world."

"No," said Regan. "The foals deserve better than to grow up hiding, and they'll hate me for it when they realize I'm the reason they had to. Chicory deserves better. All the herds do. If the Queen is hurting them, we have to stop her. You raised me to save our world. Let me save it."

There was no way to answer that, and so no one said anything, not even when Regan burst into tears and threw her arms around Pansy's waist, holding on as if her life depended on it.

PART IV

TO VISIT THE QUEEN

13 THE ROAD TO RUIN

REGAN LEFT AS THE sun was sinking low against the horizon, painting the sky in purple and orange, like a bruise that would never heal. The rest of the herd came to the edge of the wood to watch her go, even the foals, who didn't understand what was happening, only that their favorite playmate was walking away, a bundle slung over one shoulder and a bow hooked over the other, and that she wasn't looking back.

Chicory buried her face against her mother's shoulder to hide her tears. Pansy and Daisy didn't bother, only stood and let their tears run down their cheeks unchecked. None of them looked away until Regan had reached the place where the road began to bend out of sight. Bit by bit, she disappeared. One of the foals made a disbelieving wailing sound. She didn't come back.

She didn't come back.

For Regan, walking away from the forest was the most terrifying thing she'd ever done. She had been afraid before, but the fear had always been connected to consequences, not choices. Laurel's reaction to her secret had been terrifying; she didn't regret telling it, not anymore. She wasn't ashamed of herself. Laurel was the one who had been in the wrong, and anyone who answered a friend's honesty with horror and rejection had never been a friend in the first place. She'd been afraid when stepping though the illusion of a door had been enough to drop her in a strange new world, but that fear had passed and been replaced with wonder, and love, and security a long, long time ago. She wouldn't have changed it if she could have.

This, though . . . this was something she had chosen and was still choosing, with every step away from home and safety. She could run. She could hide. She could refuse to face a Queen who considered her a danger because of who and what she was. She could keep living a happy, sheltered life, protected by her herd, putting her needs above theirs. The foals would be old enough to ask about their fathers soon. They would want the company of their own kind, and they deserved to have it. Chicory deserved it, too. She deserved Fairs and a herd of her own; she deserved a courtship, if she wanted one, and a husband she'd see once a year when she chose to see him at all. They deserved normal lives.

It was ridiculous, thinking about giving normal lives to other people when she was never going to have one for herself, and Regan laughed as she walked, the sound bright and merry in the cool morning air. She was a human who preferred the company of horses, or at least creatures who looked like horses. She was a hero, or she was going to be, and she never wanted to go home, even though she knew her parents had to miss her. She chose this world, where she could never be normal, over the world she had been made for. So it was a little strange that she was so eager to give away the things she could never have, even if she tried to want them.

She was still laughing when a great, shaggy black horse rose out of the ditch next to the narrow road, water weeds tangled in its mane and pond scum dripping from its muzzle. That muzzle was slightly too pronounced for its head, and its lips bulged like they were trying to contain something no herbivore's mouth should have to hold. It looked at her with one immense brown eye. That, at least, looked like it could have belonged to a normal horse, wide and soft, the color of chocolate, and fringed with long, delicate lashes.

"I'm not coming any closer to you," Regan informed the kelpie. "And you shouldn't come any closer to me. I know what kelpies do to anything they think of as prey." She unslung the bow from her shoulder, keeping it low by her hip as she pulled an arrow from the quiver at her side. "You go your way, and I'll go mine."

The kelpie's lips pulled back from jagged teeth that would have looked equally at home in an alligator's mouth. Then it said, in a gravelly voice, "Human girl. These roads are not safe for you alone."

Regan jumped. "They never told me kelpies could *talk*," she blurted.

The kelpie tossed its head. "And they kept you away from us, so you would never have cause to learn," it said dismissively. "The centaurs are weak, and so they hate us. Civilization makes you weak. The centaurs have been civilized for long and long. If we had found you first, your time in the Hooflands would have been a very different thing."

"Yes, because you would have ripped me to pieces and devoured my liver."

"Perhaps," allowed the kelpie. "But not until the time had come for you to play at salvation. We aren't civilized, but we aren't *stupid*."

"That makes sense," said Regan, and slung her bow back over her shoulder. "Still would have been nice to know you could talk before this. You startled me."

"Other things in this forest will do worse than startle you if you keep on the way you're going," said the kelpie. "Here. Get on my back. Humans are notoriously slow, and I can have you to the castle in less time than it takes my stomach to sour."

Regan took a step backward. "If I get on your back, you'll rip me to pieces."

"Have you saved the world yet?"

"Well, no."

"Then no, I won't. I told you, I'm not *stupid*. My hunger to survive is greater than my hunger for human flesh. Especially not human flesh that's been kept by *centaurs* for years on end. You'll taste of austerity and bad cooking. No, thank you. Get on my back and I'll carry you where you need to go."

Still Regan hesitated.

The kelpie stomped one foot in the muddy puddle it was standing in.

"Don't be foolish, child. The sooner you save the world, the sooner I *can* eat you."

"Do you have a name?" asked Regan hesitantly. For once, the conviction that she had a destiny seemed to be working in her favor, if it was keeping this kelpie from eating her.

"My mother called me 'Gristle,' for she thought I would be the toughest of her children, and she was right, for of my brothers and sisters and I, I'm still here and they're long-since devoured and digested and gone to fertilize the fields. As all of us must one day do. Well, human child? Will you let me carry you?"

Regan had been living with the centaurs for five years. She could run all day and not feel tired; she could climb for hours and only want to climb some more. But she still appreciated the comfort and calm, and efficiency, of being on horseback. She didn't know if kelpies were inclined to lie in pursuit of a meal—but then, she hadn't known they could talk, either. There was a lot she didn't know. But she knew she could ride.

"Have you ever been ridden before?" she asked, approaching the kelpie.

"No," it said, and walked out of the puddle, stopping in front of her and looking at her with one arrogant brown eye.

"This may feel strange, then," she said, and planted her hands on its withers, boosting herself up in a single smooth motion, slinging her leg over the kelpie's back and settling comfortably into position. The kelpie startled, shaking its head up and down, but didn't buck. Regan grabbed its mane with both hands anyway, keeping herself from being thrown off.

"What are you *doing*?" the kelpie demanded.

"Riding you. What did you think it meant, to be ridden?"

"Not this! The weight of you, the warmth of you . . . it's unbearable." Gristle shuddered. "The centaurs must be mad, to carry you as far as they have. What did you do to them?"

"Nothing. They must have civilized themselves into putting up with it. But if you can't do as much as a centaur can, I can get down . . ."

"No!" Gristle calmed. "If the centaurs can do it, a kelpie can do it! *I* can do it! Stay where you are, human, and I will be the one who delivers our salvation to her destiny!" The kelpie took a few unsteady steps forward before breaking into a loping, ground-eating run. Regan held on as tightly as she dared, sinking into the kelpie's steady, unbroken gait, balancing herself as best she could atop the racing beast.

This was nothing like riding Chicory, who had been so careful with her in the beginning, and who had grown up with Regan on her back, until neither of them really noticed it anymore. This wasn't like riding her horse back home, either. Tracker had always been biddable, as suited a horse mostly ridden by children under the age of twelve, and while he had sometimes tried to push back against her instructions, she had always been conclusively in charge of their adventures. Not so with Gristle. The kelpie was running because *he* wanted to run, and not because of anything Regan did or asked for or wanted. All she could do was hold on and hope she didn't get thrown.

Gristle ran and ran, hooves churning divots into the fields, ran until the sun shifted in the sky and it was late in the afternoon, the light lengthening and turning soft as butter. When he finally stopped, they were in the dusky shadows of an unfamiliar forest. He gave no warning, merely froze, dropping his head, sides heaving, and said, in a voice just shy of a snarl, "Get off me now."

"What?" asked Regan. Her entire body was one big ache, from her thighs and bottom to the crown of her head.

"I said, *get off*," snarled Gristle. Startled, Regan unwound her hands from his mane—the hair had dug in deep as she clung, leaving red lines like lashes across her palms—and slid off his back, landing in a heap when her legs refused to hold her. She rolled over, propping herself up on her elbows, and looked at the kelpie.

Gristle was breathing hard, head still drooping and flecks of sweat dotting his sides. He looked exhausted. Regan hurt all over. She still levered herself to her feet, shrugged off her pack, and dug through it until she found a rag that had started existence as a piece of the jeans she'd been wearing when she stumbled through her door. It was buttery-soft, softer than denim had any right to be, worn down to threads and memory. She took a hesitant step toward Gristle, knees shaking with exhaustion and sudden fear, and when the kelpie didn't snap at her, began carefully, hesitantly wiping down his sides with the cloth.

Always take care of the horse that carries you. That was one of the first lessons she'd learned back at the stable. Chicory had never required much in the way of cosseting or currying, but Chicory had hands. Gristle had nothing of the sort. He stiffened when she began her work, lifting his head enough to cast a suspicious, narrow-eyed look in her direction, but when he realized she wasn't hurting him, he put his head down again, letting her wipe down his entire coat. She didn't have a comb, and so she began unsnarling his mane and tail with her fingernails, careful not to scratch too hard. Eventually, his head came up and stayed up, ears swiveling as he held himself perfectly still and submitted to her ministrations.

When she finally removed her hands and stepped back, he sighed, as mournfully as a man who had seen the road to paradise and been told that it was not for him to walk. "Perhaps there are some benefits to civilization after all," he said.

"I'm all gross and sweaty, and you can't clean me up," said Regan. "Is there water near here?"

Gristle looked at her. "Where there's water, you'll find kelpies. Not all my cousins are as considerate as I am."

"You mean they'll eat me before I have a chance to save the world?"

"Not all of you, but I think you'd regard losing a limb or two as inconvenient enough to make the world harder to save."

Regan laughed. "I'll be careful. Is there water?"

Gristle tossed his head. "You'd ask a kelpie if there's water? Of course there's water. It's why we've stopped here for the night. There's a lake that way." He pointed his nose toward the trees. "Deep enough to swim in, deep enough to drown in."

"I'll try to avoid the second part," said Regan, and walked into the trees, leaving the kelpie behind.

It was odd, being this far away from home with no idea how she would go about getting back there. She had known she had to leave, but she hadn't considered the homesickness that would follow, or the loneliness.

She didn't have to walk far before she stepped into a clearing dominated by a small lake. It was big enough for her to swim until her arms gave out without touching the other side. She was, or appeared to be, alone.

Dropping her things on the flat-packed ground, Regan cupped her hands around her mouth and called, "Are there any kelpies here?"

An echo caught her voice and flung it to the lake's far shore. No shaggy black heads rose out of the depths. Regan lowered her hands.

"If there are, I guess they don't want to chat," she said, and unbuckled her belt, dropping it next to her bow. Her tunic was the next to go, until she stood before the water as naked as the day she'd been born. She walked into the lake.

The water was cold, but that was no trouble; it had been five years since she'd touched water warmer than the sunlight, and it didn't bother her anymore, even when it left her blue-lipped and shivering. She waded until the lake touched her shoulders, and then she ducked under, letting it sluice through her hair and wash away the long day's journey. The chill bite of the water soothed her thoughts in tandem with her aching muscles, and she surfaced into a better world.

Assuming one could call a ring of kelpies "a better world." The water horses watched her with hungry eyes, fangs on full display and ears tight against their heads. Regan blinked. No fear followed. The centaurs had protected her too well, and Gristle had carried her too far, and she could never truly fear something that looked so much like her beloved horses.

"Hello," she said. "I'm Regan. I'm supposed to save the world, and I can't do that if you eat me."

The kelpies exchanged uncertain glances before backing away in the water, their ears coming up in curiosity. Whatever they'd been expecting from a human, it wasn't pleasantness, wasn't politeness. Regan smiled as they retreated, ducking under the water again to give her hair one more good rinsing before she began to paddle toward the shore. Several kelpies followed, although they stayed in the shallows, lurking and watching her as she got out of the water. Regan wrung the water out of her hair and turned to face them, a smile on her face.

"Thank you for not eating me," she said as Gristle came trotting through the woods. He snorted when he saw the other kelpies, and moved to put his body protectively between them and Regan. Regan put a hand on his neck, trying to soothe him.

"They didn't do anything wrong," she said. "They just came to see who was swimming in their lake."

"It's the human," said one of the kelpies. "Why is the human here? The human is supposed to be far away from here, with the centaurs, inciting the Queen's wrath."

Gristle tossed his head. "I brought her here. She *rode* me. I'm taking her to the Queen."

"To claim the bounty?" asked another kelpie, sounding confused. "What will you do with money?"

"No! To save the world!" Gristle snarled like a dog, keeping himself between Regan and the others. "She will do what she came here to do, and *then* we can devour her!"

Regan gave him a shocked look. "Did you offer to help me just so you could be the one to eat me?"

"And what if I did? I told you I would be the one to eat you! You're still being helped, and I've made no attempt to hide my nature. I am a kelpie, not some soft, *civilized* thing."

"Unbelievable." Regan began gathering her clothes from the bank, yanking them on. "And to think I groomed you after you brought me here."

"Where are you going, human?"

"To find a tree I can sleep in. I'll be safe there." She wasn't actually sure. Perytons couldn't climb, but they could fly, and they were meat-eaters as much as the kelpies were. She gave the kelpie a withering look as she picked up her things. "You can sleep with the roots if you don't want to lose sight of me."

She spun and stalked into the wood. A moment later she heard hoofbeats moving behind her, and smiled, knowing that Gristle was following. She wouldn't be spending the night alone.

It didn't take long to find a suitable tree. She reached up to grab the lowest branch and began pulling herself up, climbing with the casual ease of long practice. When she finally looked down, Gristle was standing by the tree, watching her.

"This is normal for humans?" he asked.

"We're pretty arboreal, yeah," she said, and kept climbing until she had reached a branch long and broad enough for her to stretch out on, letting her arms dangle. "Adult humans don't climb as much, but for children, climbing is a natural instinct."

"Like eating is for kelpies," said Gristle. He sounded relieved. "You don't fight your nature. You can't expect me to fight mine."

"I suppose I can't," said Regan thoughtfully. "But you have to swear not to eat me until after I've done whatever I have to do to save the world."

"You have my word," he said.

"Good." She hung her bow from a nearby branch, tucked her pack under her head, and closed her eyes, and everything was silence as girl and kelpie slept.

14 THROUGH THE WOODS

REGAN WOKE TO THE brush of feathers against her cheek. She opened her eyes and sat up, all too aware that she'd spent the night in a tree and the slightest wrong move could send her toppling to the ground. Then she shrieked.

The young peryton perched on the end of the branch screamed and fumbled backward, wings flailing. At the base of the tree, Gristle snarled, the sound of a large predator whose territory had been threatened. Regan scrambled away on her hands, stopping when her back hit the trunk. She huddled there, panting, as the peryton stopped flailing and stared at her with enormous eyes the color of a cloudless sky.

"What are you *doing*?" Regan demanded.

"I thought you might be dead!" said the peryton, in high-pitched but perfectly understandable English. "You weren't moving, and there was a kelpie at the base of the tree. I thought it was scavenging! I'm sorry, I'm sorry, don't eat me!"

"But you were planning to eat *me*," said Regan. Then she blinked. "Perytons can talk?"

"Everything talks, human," said Gristle. "Even worthless feathered scavengers. Most simply can't listen. You'd have heard our kind long ago if you hadn't been with the centaurs."

"I'm not worthless," protested the peryton. "I hunt, and I fly, and I feed my parcel!"

"Worthless," repeated Gristle.

"Don't fight," said Regan. Focusing on the peryton, she asked, "Are you still going to eat me?"

"Not while you're alive! That would be awful!" The peryton flattened her ears, looking distressed. "Please don't hurt me."

"I wouldn't," said Regan. "I don't think I *could*. You have wings and antlers and very sharp hooves. I only have a bow."

"And thumbs, and a kelpie," said the peryton.

To Regan's surprise, Gristle didn't protest the idea that Regan had him, just continued to prowl around the base of the tree and occasionally snarl. Moving cautiously, she slipped her pack over her shoulders, grabbed her bow, and began climbing down to where Gristle waited.

To her further surprise, the peryton followed, flapping its great barn owl's wings and gliding to a dainty landing, keeping a respectful distance from Gristle. She looked at Regan and said, "You're the human. I'd heard that you existed, but I never thought to see you."

"We're off to seek her destiny," said Gristle. "She'll save the world, and then I'll eat her."

"I don't like that second part," said Regan. "I may not like the first part, either. I'm not sure yet. I don't believe in destiny, and I don't want to disappear, whether it's because I've been eaten or because my job's done."

The peryton looked uncertain, or as uncertain as a creature with a face like a skinless deer could look. She swung her head back and forth between Regan and Gristle, studying them both, before she finally said, "I'm coming with you."

"No," said Gristle.

"Are you sure that's a good idea?" asked Regan.

"My name is Zephyr, and I'm coming with you," said the peryton. "I'm a strong flyer. I can see things neither of you can see, grounded creatures that you are. I can make this easier for you, and I can be part of saving the world. No peryton has ever been a part of saving the world before. I'll be a legend, and then they'll have to let me have a parcel of my own, stags and does and fawns and all the forest stretched before us like a gift." She half-spread her wings, tone blissful.

"Fine," said Regan, before Gristle could object. She slung her bow back over her shoulder and turned to the kelpie. "Do you know how much farther we need to go?"

"Just to the line of the horizon," muttered the kelpie. "We'll be there by sundown."

"Then we go," said Regan, with more certainty than she felt. "The three of us." She walked to Gristle, boosting herself onto the kelpie's back and digging her hands into his mane. "For the Hooflands."

"For the Hooflands," said Gristle, and took off at a gallop, leaving Zephyr to flap frantically as she struggled to keep up.

In moments, it was like they'd never been there at all.

15 IT TAKES SO LONG TO REACH THE INEVITABLE

THE OUTLINE OF THE castle appeared on the horizon as the sun was dipping lower in the sky, casting long shadows across the fields. It was not as crenelated and precise as a castle from a fairy tale, but was rough-hewn and imposing, as if the rocks had simply fallen from the sky and piled themselves into the shape of a castle, without any sapient intervention. Gristle slowed, gallop becoming a canter, becoming a trot, finally becoming a walk. Zephyr landed and walked beside him, although far enough away that he couldn't easily bite or strike her.

Regan sat up straighter on Gristle's back, untangling her hands from his mane and wincing at the new lines his hair had cut into her palms. "Is that it?" she asked.

Gristle snorted. "No, we're going to a different castle. Of course that's it. The Queen's castle now. The King's castle once. Hoof to hoof, hand to hand, back to the beginning of the Hooflands."

"I think I can walk from here," said Regan. Gristle stopped, and she slid down from his back, stretching to work out the kinks in her spine. Then she began walking toward the castle, with Gristle pacing her on one side and Zephyr on the other. Their hooves clopped softly against the soft earth, and the sky smelled like rain on the way, and everything about the moment was inevitable; everything about the moment had been coming for her since the moment she'd walked through a door that wasn't and into a world that somehow knew enough to know that it was going to need saving.

Not just saving: saving by someone who loved it. If the door had opened now, today, and dropped a gangly, long-limbed Regan wearing fresh new jeans and smelling of her mother's perfume into the field, she wouldn't have been fit for saving anything at all. She had never been given the opportunity to become that version of herself, but she knew in her heart that the other Regan wasn't somehow the better one. The other Regan would never have understood the simple joy of fishing in the lake during her morning bath, hooking fat, slow bass under the gills with her fingers and flipping them onto the shore. She wouldn't have seen the colts growing up, or lain with Chicory in fields of sweet grass, wondering about the shape of the future. If she was going to save the Hooflands, she had to be this version of herself, this awkward, half-wild, uncertain girl who'd grown up on a centaur's back, racing through woods and breathing in air that always smelled, ever so faintly, of horsehair and hay. That other Regan had been the first sacrifice necessary to save the world, and she had made it without even knowing, and still she had no regrets.

She still didn't believe in destiny. Clay shaped into a cup was not always destined to become a drinking vessel; it was simply shaped by someone too large to be resisted. She was not clay, but she had been shaped by her circumstances all the same, not directed by any destiny.

Regan walked on toward the castle, which loomed larger and larger before her, until it dominated the line of the sky. "Was she always a bad queen?" she asked. "Do either of you know?"

"The only bad thing I've ever heard of her doing was burning the centaur fields to the south," said Zephyr. "She tried to take the human from them shortly after it arrived— I'm sorry, tried to take you—and when her people failed, she ordered the hippocampi to carry burning brands and set alight everything the centaurs owned, to punish them for disobeying her."

Regan, who had heard nothing of this, stiffened but forced herself to keep walking. All these things had happened years ago, and she couldn't change them now. All she could do was try to keep them from happening again. All she could do was keep moving.

"All queens are bad queens," said Gristle. "When the queen is a centaur or a faun, they treat those of us without hands as if we were somehow less a part of the Hooflands than they are, when the very world is named for us. When the queen is a kirin or a hippogriff, they behave as if those who eat meat are savages who don't deserve the lands we live on. There's never been a kelpie queen. Those doors are closed to monsters like me."

"There's never been a peryton queen, either," said Zephyr sadly. "They call us monsters, too, because they can't talk to us."

"Why can't they?" asked Regan, confused. "If I can talk to you, they should be able to."

"Civilized people don't know how to listen," said Gristle. "All their magic goes into the places they believe it belongs. You, human, have been here long enough to learn some magic of your own, and now any of us can speak with you, if we have cause to want to."

Regan blinked slowly. "Oh," she said.

"It won't make the centaurs stop thinking of us as monsters," said Zephyr. "There will never be a peryton queen."

"But that's not fair," protested Regan. "How does a queen get chosen, anyway?"

"When an old queen dies, every herd in the Hooflands puts forth their finest candidate. They go to the meeting chamber built by the first Alliance of Hooves and Hands, back in the days before we had memory or thought, when the humans came here and refused to claim our pastures as their own. Only one leaves the chamber and ascends to the throne. The others are lost forever."

"One of my mother's sisters went when this queen was chosen, even though she knew a peryton would never hold the throne," said Zephyr, sounding almost wistful. "I never met her, but Mother says she had antlers like cupped hands, full of wind and moonlight, and she was beautiful beyond bearing."

Regan didn't feel like she could say anything about peryton standards of beauty, so she didn't say anything at all.

"As to how the queen is chosen from among the candidates, no one knows," said Gristle. "Maybe she eats the others. Maybe she takes the throne with a full belly, containing part of every other thinking creature in the Hooflands. Even if she doesn't eat them, they all vanish utterly and eternally."

Regan shuddered. "But that would mean every reign began with murder. That's no way to start."

"We know she's a bad queen now, so maybe she was always bad and just took a while to show it," said Zephyr.

"Yes, but if she killed all the other contenders, then all the other kings and queens before her had to do that too. And if they all had to do that, there have never been any good rulers."

"You're starting to understand!" said Gristle, sounding proud of himself. "You'll be a wonderful dinner, after you've saved the world. Wisdom seasons the meat."

"I'm not meat, I'm Regan," said Regan. The castle wall was in front of them now. It was a smooth unbroken gray, the stones stacked so carefully that there was scarcely a seam between them. Regan kept walking, paralleling the wall, until she saw a place where the stones didn't quite fit. They gapped, not much, not enough for even Zephyr, who was slim, with her doe's body, to fit through.

But it was wide enough for Regan.

"Thank you," she said, turning to face both the strange creatures who had become her traveling companions. "I wouldn't have made it this far, this fast, without you. But now it's time for me to keep going on my own."

"Let me check first to be sure it's safe," said Zephyr, and

launched herself into the air before Regan could object. The peryton gained height with surprising speed, banking and wheeling above the castle walls, and perhaps there were advantages to being thought of as an unthinking monster, because no one raised any alarms at her presence. Regan stayed where she was, watching her fly, suddenly understanding how a peryton could be considered beautiful. Zephyr was lovely in the air.

When Zephyr landed again, she shook her head, like she was chasing away the last slivers of the wind, and said, "There are guards in the high battlements, but they won't see you if you enter from down here. Your way is clear."

"Thank you," said Regan again. "I'm ready to continue."

"Good luck," said Zephyr.

Gristle didn't say anything at all, only watched as Regan turned sideways and squeezed into the break in the wall. He stayed there, silently watching the space where she had been, until Zephyr spread her wings and leapt back into the air, and he was alone. He paced a circle, then lay down in the grass, head resting on his forelegs, and waited.

Inside the wall, everything was darkness and stone, pressing down on Regan until it felt like there was no air left, and she would surely suffocate and be forgotten. Would the door that caught her in the first place go hunting for another human child to sweep away, leaving them here to save the world? Or would that take too long? She was supposed to save the world, but the world had done just fine for five years while she was happily running through the woods.

She worked her way deeper into the narrow tunnel, until

every trace of light was gone and she was simply squeezing her way into infinite shadow. Just as she thought she could go no farther, her questing hand hit open air, and she was able to force her way out of the wall, into the cool, draft-ridden open space beyond.

Still there was no light. Regan grimaced, put her hands in front of herself, and began feeling her way gingerly through the darkness, stopping when her foot struck what felt like the base of a stairway. They were deep, narrow stairs, cut to suit a human's tread, and not the longer stride of a centaur or kelpie or other four-legged creature. It was strange, but not strange enough to keep her from feeling around until she found a bannister and beginning to pull herself up into the darkness.

It had been long enough since she'd had cause to climb a flight of stairs that she stumbled several times, catching her toes against the steps, nearly falling into the dark. How many other aspects of being human had she allowed to slip away from her while she was running through the forest? It was an impossible question, and so she kept going without stopping to answer it. The light began to return, a little bit at a time, the world going from utter blackness to gradients of gray, still dark at first, but thinning, until she could see her own hands, until she could see the carved shape of the bannister winding its way upward, into the highest reaches of the castle.

Regan kept pressing onward, until the light was bright enough to read by, until the stairs leveled out at a small landing, connected to a long hall. Unslinging her bow from her shoulder, she swallowed hard and walked on.

The air in the castle was cold and stale, nothing like what

she expected from a palace. It should have been warm and bright and filled with life, scented with cake and tea and other delicacies. This didn't feel like walking into a castle. It felt like walking into a tomb.

The thing about walking into a tomb is that it leaves plenty of time to consider what a foolish idea that is. As she walked, Regan remembered Pansy telling her about Queen Kagami, back when she'd first arrived in the Hooflands.

Regan stopped.

According to Pansy, Queen Kagami had been assisted in reclaiming her family's castle from a wicked kelpie king by the last human to come to the Hooflands. But Zephyr and Gristle agreed that a kelpie had never held the throne, and said the crown was passed by a challenge, not along family lines. Why would they lie to her? Why would *Pansy*, who was a second mother now, have lied to her? Unless the centaurs weren't lying, just mistaken—but then why did they have one history of the Hooflands, while the kelpies and perytons had another? It made no sense.

It made no sense unless Gristle and Zephyr told the truth when they said that there was one set of rules for the people who agreed that they were people, and another for the monsters who everyone else agreed couldn't be people at all. It made no sense unless the Hooflands had been unfair since the very beginning.

"I can hear you breathing," called a voice from somewhere up ahead of her, old as the grave and dry as dust. "Come in, little intruder. Come in. I've been waiting for you. I've been waiting for *so long*."

Regan had never seen a kirin, but from what she remembered, they were shaped much like unicorns, with hooves and horns and long, equine muzzles instead of flat human faces. The voice had none of the faint lisp she was accustomed to hearing from equine lips. The voice was low and tired and ancient, and entirely indistinguishable from a human's. Cautiously, Regan started walking again, suddenly deeply glad for the bow in her hand.

A door stood open a little distance down the hall. Regan peeked around the frame, into the room on the other side.

It was large and square, with tapestries on the walls and carpets on the floor. A fire crackled in the grate, struggling and failing to warm the space. At the center of the room, positioned well away from the walls, was a tall canopy bed, mounded with pillows, and at the center of the bed was a human man, his hair grown long and wispy to match his unkempt beard and mustache. His body was so slight and wasted that it barely made a shape beneath the covers, which might as well have been tucked down flat.

He met Regan's eyes, lifting his head the barest fraction of an inch in the process, and smiled.

"Took you long enough," he said.

16 THE DANGER OF DESTINY

"I EXPECTED YOU YEARS ago," the man continued. "I thought you'd do what I did, and make the first person you met bring you straight here, assuming you could see them as a person. I thought you'd be eager to get down to the business of heroism and fulfilling your destiny. Not to run off to the woods and live like an animal. I suppose I shouldn't make assumptions." He coughed, covering his mouth with his hand; when he pulled it away, his palm was red with blood. "But you're here now, come to save the world the same way I did."

Regan stared at him. "I thought you disappeared after you helped Kagami take the throne," she said, lips numb.

"Is that what they say? Well, I suppose it's a better story than 'I slit a silly little mare's throat and bled her out in what she thought was going to be her throne room.'" His voice was cold, dispassionate; not cruel. He would have had to care at least a little to be cruel. "I was seventeen years old. I had a lover waiting for me, a farm I was set to take over when my father died, and suddenly, these talking horses were tell-ing me I had to be their savior, even though there wasn't anything to save them *from*. Kagami was the one who found me after I tumbled through my door. She said the king had ordered her family's fields burned when they refused to pay their taxes, and so she thought saving the world might mean overthrowing the king. It was as good an answer as any. She took me here, to the palace, and I learned the king had been dead for decades, and an ancient human woman had been secretly ruling in his place, never showing her face to the representatives of the herds who came to call on her, never stirring from the palace. She was even older then than I am now, if you can believe it." He coughed again, almost smiling. "I had never seen anyone so old. It seemed impossi-ble that she should be among the living. She had been here since she was a child, speaking to her subjects from behind a curtain, and had been waiting for me for years."

"You killed her," whispered Regan.

"Yes, I did," said the man. "She told me how to operate this palace from the shadows, and I killed her at her request, and then I killed Kagami, before she could go back to her farm and tell the others that their beloved king had been a human woman all along. That was how I saved the world. I took the old woman's place behind the curtain. They all believe the Queen's splendor is too glorious for any of her subjects to behold, and they're happy to obey a voice without a face when it tells them to do things they already believe to be correct."

Regan blinked, disbelieving. "How did murder save the world?"

"They believe humans are heroes. They believe they're ruled by one of their own kind. Their world is built on those beliefs. They couldn't survive learning they were wrong. It would destroy their entire system of governance, such as it is. So I did as she asked, and I freed her from their expectations. Then I put Kagami down like the animal she was, and sat back to wait for my door to return." His expression darkened. "It didn't. It left me here, alone, apart from my own people, to grow old and fade away in a world full of beasts, yoked to a throne I couldn't abandon without revealing what I'd done and destroying the illusion. At first I kept my place because I wanted to keep my word to the woman I had killed, and then I did it because being old and alone in a world of beasts was so much worse than being their queen. So I stopped waiting for the door and started waiting for you, and now here you are, my salvation."

"I'm not here to save you." Regan took a step backward. "You tried to have me kidnapped. You hurt my family."

"You mean the centaurs you've been living with? They're animals, beasts. They don't feel the way we do. They don't love the way we do." He scoffed. "Nothing I did to them had to happen. It was your fault, for not coming to me when you were first called into this world. If you'd been a better hero, none of this suffering would have taken place."

"And what was I supposed to do when I got here, kill you? I was a *child*. I still am." Regan shook her head in disgust.

"I'm not killing anyone. I don't want to be a hero. I was willing to save the Hooflands from a wicked queen if there was no one else to do the job, but I'm not willing to kill a man, not even a bad man. Destiny doesn't exist. You got it wrong. Everyone here got it wrong."

"You're a child, and I'm not!" he yelled, with all the fury his wasted body could contain. He sat up partially in the bed, then fell back into the pillows, panting. "I was so young. I had my whole future waiting for me. I had my beautiful Elise waiting for me. And I spent my entire life here, in a place I didn't belong, all for the sake of a bunch of animals and some stories they made up about how the world works. Now I'm asking a stranger to kill me and take my place, because that's what humans *do* in the Hooflands!"

"What happened to the others?" Regan's question was abrupt.

The man looked away, refusing to meet her eyes. "What others?"

"The ones who wanted the throne."

"Dead," he said. "Bones at the bottom of the castle's foundations. They walked to their dooms willingly, with thoughts of power and privilege clouding their minds. Don't mourn for them. They died generations ago."

"I thought you'd say that," said Regan, and cocked an arrow, and fired.

She had been in the woods for five years, hunting to fill her own belly and the bellies of her family. Her arrow flew straight and true, embedding itself in the headboard of the bed where the old man lay. He turned to look at it, mouth hanging slack and surprised.

"You missed," he said.

"I didn't," she replied, and turned her back on him, preparing to walk away.

"Wait!" he yelled. "You can't leave me here!"

"You'll die soon enough, from the looks of you," she said. "I apprenticed to a healer. There's blood on your hands. Your lungs are killing you, and I don't feel the need to make it any easier."

"But whoever comes to find you will find me, and they'll know about the lie! They'll know Kagami was never queen, and they'll know you're not a hero."

"Good. Let them learn that destiny's a lie, and let them find the way to govern themselves, as they should have done from the beginning. Let them learn humans are people, the way you never learned that they were," said Regan, and turned on her heel and walked away from the old man—away from the old monster—without a backward glance. She didn't feel like a hero. She didn't feel like much of anything beyond an exhausted teenager. She still felt like she was saving the world.

In the forest, she knew, her family was waiting for her. Maybe Chicory would be the next queen. The people of the Hooflands would have to decide how queens were chosen, now that they got to do it for themselves again. Maybe there was a record somewhere in the castle, some old ritual or line of succession for the people of the Hooflands to follow. Or maybe they'd decide not to have a monarch at all. The old man couldn't have done much to rule them on a day-to-day basis, not while keeping his terrible secret safe. They could set the prices of their goods themselves, and not burn anyone's fields.

At the end of the hall, Regan found another human-scaled flight of stairs, descending down along a well-lit hall lined with burning torches. Someone must have lit them. The man behind her wouldn't have had the strength. So she slung her bow back over her shoulder, squared her shoulders, and began her descent.

The stairs seemed to go on for the better part of forever, or maybe it just felt that way because she'd made so much of her climb in the dark, and was so tired now. Just as she thought she could go no farther, she heard voices ahead of her, raised in argument. She found the strength to walk faster, and reached the bottom of the stairs, whipping around the corner to see a faun, a silene, and a minotaur facing each other. The faun was holding a rope, the end of which was tied around the neck of a familiar-looking kelpie. Gristle's head was bowed, eyes on the floor. None of them were looking at Regan, whose bare feet were silent against the stone floor.

"—lurking around the castle wall," said the silene. His voice was familiar. He had no pies to offer, but Regan remembered him all the same. Her stomach soured as she realized who the minotaur must be. "There was a peryton as well, but the filthy thing flew away. We have to tell the Queen!"

So even the old human's servants thought he was Queen

Kagami? That fit with what he'd said about how none of them were ever allowed to look upon the Queen's majesty, but it still seemed odd to Regan that none of them would ever have demanded to see the Queen. Or maybe not. The old man had spoken of a curtain that sustained his pretty lie. There had been at least two humans secretly in control of the Hooflands. Maybe there had been more. Maybe this was how things had been since the beginning, with people falling through doors and believing they knew better than the people who were already there, all because they thought humans were the best possible thing to be. Maybe no one had ever seen a king or queen once they took their throne.

Regan cleared her throat.

Gristle raised his head as the three servants of the imaginary queen whipped around to stare at her. "It's the human," said the silene she recognized, in a faintly baffled tone. "How did the human get in here?"

"Queen Kagami is dead," said Regan. It was true enough, even if it wasn't the entire truth. "Let my companion go."

The silene dropped the rope. Gristle trotted over to Regan, stopping close enough that she could feel the heat coming off his hide.

"Good girl," he said approvingly. "Have you saved us all?"

"Maybe," said Regan, gently untying the rope from around Gristle's neck. Hands were useful things, from time to time. "I don't know. I think you're going to have to do some of the work to save yourselves this time." She kept looking calmly at the three servants of the Queen. "Well?" she asked. "Aren't you going to arrest me?"

"No," said the minotaur, and bowed. "She ordered us to do things in her name that the Hooflands may never forgive us for. She reigned too long, and became no fit queen. We should not have waited for a human to save us."

"I think you're right," said Regan. "And I think all people in the Hooflands should have the same rights and respect, no matter who or what they are. Humans and kelpies, centaurs and perytons, it doesn't matter. We're all people here. We all get to have the same chance to save the world."

She placed her hand on the side of Gristle's neck. His mane was still wet, as kelpies' manes always were. He flicked an ear and drew back his lips, showing her his carnivore's teeth.

"I swore to eat you when your task was finished," he said. "If you've saved us, we have no more need for a human."

"You never needed a human," she said. "We were only ever something you *wanted*, whether or not we were supposed to be here. I don't think you need me now, but I want to go home. I don't want to be eaten."

"It's a kelpie's nature to consume," said Gristle. "I've never tasted human flesh."

"Climb the stairs, then," said Regan, who was too weary to keep a secret she had never asked for and didn't believe in. "You might find something you'll like."

Gristle gave her a thoughtful look before he turned and walked away, the sound of his hoofbeats resonating off the stairwell walls. They were uneven, hampered by the shallowness of the steps, but they still echoed steadily. Regan let out an exhausted sigh and turned back to the Queen's servants.

"Where's the exit?" she asked.

The minotaur pointed. "Why do you speak to the kelpie?" he asked.

"Because I'm polite enough to listen," said Regan. Then she nodded. "Thank you," she said politely, and walked in the direction he had indicated, and once again, she did not look back.

EPILOGUE
THROUGH A DOOR TO DAMNATION

REGAN HAD BEEN IN the Hooflands long enough, racing in and out of the cottage she shared with her family, that she had lost much of her caution around doors. Perhaps that explains why she didn't see the words scratched into the frame above the door that would lead her out of the castle, back to the fields beyond. "Be Sure," the door entreated. And in that moment, Regan wasn't.

She opened the door. She stepped through.

Her hand was still on the edge of the door when the smell of exhaust hit her like a memory from a past she had almost forgotten, stinging her nose and wrenching a cough from her throat before she could stop it. The shock was enough that she lost her grip on the doorframe and fell forward, landing on her knees in the soft mud beside the creek. She heard a slam behind her, the sound of a door closing, as loud as a church bell, as final as an executioner's axe, but she didn't look back. She pressed her hands into the mud, leaning forward until her hair fell to cover her eyes, and sobbed, the great, braying sobs of a child who had been betrayed. She could feel the pollution of her home world working its way back into her lungs, where it had always belonged; she could taste the transition on her lips.

She was back. Not home; this wasn't home anymore, and hadn't been for a very long time. But back, like a rock kicked up by a centaur's hooves, left to tumble where it would.

Regan sobbed until she had no tears left in her. Then she rose, wiping mud on her tunic, and took stock of what she had. She had her bow; she had the bag on her back, with its traveling rations and precious survival supplies; she had her legs, which had carried her so far, and would gladly carry her farther if that was what she demanded of them.

The path running along the creek hadn't changed. It was still overgrown with brush and briar, still shadowed by looming trees. Regan began to walk. It was surprisingly easy once she got started. She wiped tears and snot from her face as she squished mud between her toes and followed the long arc of the path, until finally, she saw the familiar shape of a human house through the trees.

It would have been natural for her to break into a run at the promise of seeing her parents, who she had never stopped loving, even if she had stopped wanting to go back to them. But she knew that once she stepped inside, everything would change, and she wouldn't have the power to change it back. So she walked slowly across the field to the back porch. An unfamiliar car was parked in the driveway. A very familiar black-and-white cat was curled, sleeping, on the porch swing.

Regan reached for the doorknob, after first looking closely at every inch of the door itself. There was nothing written there. The knob turned easily in her hand.

She opened the door.

She stepped inside.